Leave It to Beaver

Leave It to Beaver

Authorized Edition based on the
well-known television series

by COLE FANNIN

illustrated by
ADAM SZWEJKOWSKI

WHITMAN PUBLISHING COMPANY
Racine, Wisconsin

CONTENTS

1 The Markley Gold Mine   11

2 Beaver Takes Off   24

3 Trouble With Kit   38

4 A Car of His Own   52

5 False Alarm!   67

6 Beaver's Big Job   82

7 Bad News for Wally   96

8 Getting Rich   111

9 Aggie's Story   123

10 Too Much to Bear   137

11 Kit Disappears   152

12 Flood!   165

13 A Witness for Wally   181

14 Beaver Makes Up His Mind   196

1

The Markley
Gold Mine

The spring day when Theodore Cleaver, known to nearly everybody as Beaver, fell down the old mine began about like any other day.

He got up, brushed his teeth, washed, argued with his older brother Wally, dressed himself, and went down to breakfast. He couldn't argue with Wally there, but he started in again as soon as they returned to their room.

"You know what I'm going to be when I grow up?" Beaver asked. "The richest man in the world, that's what! And when anybody ever comes around and asks me for something, I'm going to say, 'Go away!' "

Wally, who was several years older than

Beaver, and in high school, said, "Beave, I just
don't have any money to lend you. When I told
you I was broke, I meant that I've spent every
cent of my allowance for this week."

Beaver thought this over. He said hopefully,
"Maybe you can lend me something when you
get your allowance next week?"

"Sure, if there is any to spare," Wally said. "But
I'm afraid it won't be very much. Listen, you
ought to forget that bicycle you keep talking
about."

Wally was looking at his face in the mirror.
He certainly had been looking at his face a lot
lately.

"Gosh, I can't forget about it!" Beaver said.
"S'pose somebody sees it in Mr. Hallam's window
and goes in and buys the bike? That would be
awful!"

The subject of their discussion was an English
bicycle, all blue and silver, that Beaver wanted
more than he had ever wanted anything.

He said, "Maybe Dad would lend me the

money and I could pay him back out of my allowance, a little bit at a time!"

"Twenty-one dollars? That would take you years, with the size of your allowance, even if Dad was willing, and I don't think he would be," Wally said. "Listen, Beave, I can't understand why you're getting so worked up over an old bike. If it was only a car, instead—"

A knock sounded on their door, interrupting him. Then it opened and Ward Cleaver stepped in. He was their father. "Let's go, men," he said. "I'm due at the office, and you two are due at school."

"Hey, Dad, I think I've got one!" Wally suddenly cried. "Right here! I'm sure of it!"

He was pointing at his upper lip. Ward Cleaver stepped closer and gravely examined it.

"No, son," he said at last. "It's just another false alarm. You haven't started to grow a mustache yet. And for heaven's sake don't be in such a hurry to begin shaving."

"Aw, gee, Dad." Wally grumbled. "Sometimes

you talk as though you don't want me to ever grow up!"

"Not at all. Just don't try to do it so infernally fast," his father said. "Everybody out now."

Wally hurriedly combed his hair again, about the tenth time he had done that since getting up, Beaver thought, and they all went downstairs together.

Mom was waiting for them at the front door.

Dad was tall and dark-haired, young-looking and nearly always smiling. He was, Beaver had long ago decided, just about the best dad that anybody had ever had. But Mom, of course, was something very special.

She was slender and pretty, with fluffy blond hair. She always smelled so nice, had soft cool hands and a gentle voice—and it constantly surprised Beaver that she knew so much about boys, considering the fact that she had never been one herself.

Her name was June Cleaver.

Mom kissed Wally on the cheek, and he left.

She inspected Beaver's face and neck and ears and hands, smoothed back a thick lock of dark hair from his forehead, and handed him his lunch, then kissed him, too.

Beaver did not care very much for that. But Wally had once said, "All mothers like to kiss their sons—because it makes them feel good, I suppose. And Mom does so much for us that I don't think we ought to mind."

"Yeah, I guess so," Beaver had agreed. "She's a pretty good mom."

He knew she was a lot more than that, but felt too shy and tongue-tied to say so.

She didn't fuss over him now, just said, "Good-bye, Beaver," and gave him a little pat as he went out the door. She would kiss Dad now, and not on the cheek, either. Dad never seemed to mind at all.

Wally was half a block away already, heading toward the high school with his two closest friends, Eddie Haskell and Lumpy Rutherford. Sometimes it seemed to Beaver that he just couldn't wait until he was in high school, too. Wally was going out for the track team and joining clubs and doing all sorts of exciting things.

Beaver had tried to learn everything that Wally was doing, but Wally had said, in a lofty manner, "Ah, you wouldn't understand, Beave, you're not old enough yet. Besides, there's a lot of secret stuff in those clubs that I'm not supposed to tell anybody."

Doggone being a kid brother anyway, Beaver thought, starting to kick a can along the sidewalk.

He turned left at the first corner. His school was five blocks away and Beaver walked to it because Dad thought the exercise was good for him. He liked walking to school. There were so many interesting things to see and do.

First, he came to where a ditch-digging machine was at work scooping out a ditch for something and had to watch that for a while. Then he decided to detour a bit and go by the fire station.

Beaver visited the fire station at every opportunity. Captain Gus, who was the boss there, was sitting out in front, tilted back in a chair with a cap down over his eyes. General, beside him, greeted Beaver with a thump of his tail. General was a dog, a Dalmatian. Beaver had never been able to figure out whether he was white with black spots or black with white spots.

Captain Gus pushed back his cap. He was old and white-haired, with twinkly blue eyes, and Beaver thought of him as just about his best grown-up friend. "Good morning, Beaver Cleaver," he said. "General and I have missed you for the last couple of days."

"I've been sort of busy, Captain Gus," Beaver said. Then he looked at the big red truck in the fire house and added, "The pumper sure is shiny today!"

"Thank you," Captain Gus said. "I think it would be just a mite shinier, though, if you had been here to help us polish it. Maybe you can come by on Saturday, and we'll make the pumper really sparkle!"

"I sure will!" Beaver agreed eagerly.

"Don't you forget," Captain Gus told him.

Beaver went on, resisting the temptation to go a couple of blocks out of his way now, past Mr. Hallam's shop, so he could look at the bicycle again. He decided to take a short cut to school through the hollow.

This was a fairly wide ravine with some trees at one side, and a little creek which sometimes flooded the south end of town when there was a hard rain. At the other side of the hollow there was a big old house which had been closed up, with the windows boarded over, as long as Beaver could remember.

Mom had once said that the town ought to do something about the hollow. "It's a disgrace with those squatters at the north end!" she had exclaimed.

She had meant some poor people living in shanties they had built north of the big old house.

Dad had said, "But the town can't do anything since the squatters are beyond the city limits. Anyway, all of the hollow belongs to the Markleys, and doing something about the squatters would be up to them."

"I wonder if Bob and Enid Markley will ever come back to their big house to live?" Mom had said.

"No telling," Dad had replied. "The last I heard, they were living at a hotel in San Francisco."

There was a bridge over the hollow, but Beaver slid down a steep bank, went through some trees, and crossed the creek by skipping from rock to rock. There wasn't much water in the creek. A mile south of the bridge it ran into Hazy River. Then Beaver came to the steep ravine bank on the opposite side of the hollow and discovered that the mine there was no longer closed up.

It was a sort of hole in the bank, and always before it had been boarded over, with a sign painted on one of the boards in crooked letters, which read: MARKLEY GOLD MINE. EVERYBODY KEEP OUT. BEEWARE!

The first time Beaver had seen it, he had

excitedly reported to his father, who had snorted and said, "There isn't any gold within a thousand miles of here and that isn't a mine—just a hole Bob Markley and his brothers dug one summer. It should have been filled in years ago. I think you should stay away from there, son."

Beaver had no intention of taking any chances now. But the boards had been pulled away, the hole in the bank was open, and he felt a powerful itch to take a look into it. He put down his books and lunch, then cautiously approached, really not meaning to go too close.

And all at once it happened; the ground seemed to slide from under his feet. He tried to grab at something, but there was nothing to grab. Then he was in the hole, slipping and sliding, unable to stop himself.

It angled into the bank instead of going straight down, so that Beaver felt like he was sliding down a staircase with no steps. But then, suddenly, the hole did go straight down. Beaver slid over a ledge and fell a distance of five or six

feet, and landed hard, with a bump, at the bottom.

He wasn't hurt and scrambled quickly to his feet.

There was a little light from above, but it was still sort of dark and scary. Beaver looked around. He reached up, but the ledge was too high above him. Then he tried to find some fingerholds so he could climb out of the hole, but the sides were too smooth.

He yelled. "H-Hey! Somebody!"

What happened next was pretty surprising. There was a sudden cry from above and somebody else came sliding down and into the hole beside Beaver. In fact, Beaver had to jump fast to keep from being hit.

He discovered the newcomer was another boy, somebody he had never seen before, all dressed up in what looked like his best clothes. He apparently had come too close to the hole and also had fallen in.

Beaver helped him up. "Who're you?" he demanded.

"I-I'm Kit Markley," the boy said. He was as tall as Beaver, looked to be about the same age but was thinner, with light-colored hair.

It sounded as though he was about to cry. "I don't like this place," he said. "I want to get out of here!"

"Well, so do I," Beaver said. "So I guess we'd better do some yelling."

He shouted, "Help!"

Kit Markley cried, "Mama! Papa!"

There was no reply. They yelled a few more times, but nobody came along.

Kit Markley sniffled. Beaver felt almost like crying, too. But that was for little kids. He swallowed hard a couple of times and managed to keep from behaving like a baby.

He couldn't help a sinking feeling in his stomach, though. Maybe nobody would ever come along, Beaver thought. Maybe they would always be down in this hole, and his folks never would know what had happened to him.

2
Beaver Takes Off

Beaver's father had once told him that if he ever got into a tight spot the thing to do was not to waste time being scared but to keep his head and try to figure a way out. This was what he did now.

"Listen," he told the other boy, "you get down on your hands and knees. I'll stand on your back and maybe I can reach high enough to get hold of something and shinny out of here."

"Why should I be the one to get down on my hands and knees?" Kit Markley demanded. "My folks own this place. I ought to have the right to stand on your back!"

"Well," Beaver said, looking him over, "I kind

24

of think that maybe I can shinny better than you can."

"You'll go off and leave me!" the boy said.

"Why would I want to do a thing like that? Doggone it, get down on your hands and knees!"

Kit Markley grumbled, but obeyed him. Beaver climbed on his back and reached as high as he could. "Straighten up a little," he directed.

He then managed to get an elbow over the ledge at the top of the hole and, by squirming and twisting, pulled himself up onto the incline. After that, it wasn't difficult to crawl out, being very careful not to slide back down again. The boy below was yelling constantly at Beaver not to go off and leave him.

Just as Beaver emerged into daylight a man who looked to be about as old as his father came hurrying toward him. "Did you fall in there?" he demanded. "I had a feeling I should close that thing up again!"

Then the boy below let out another yell, and he started. "That's Kit!" the man said.

"Yes, sir," Beaver said. "He fell in, too. I guess we ought to do something about getting him out."

"I'll handle it," the man told him.

He had to scrunch down, sliding into the shaft that slanted into the ravine bank. A couple of minutes later he reappeared, helping the other boy out. Beaver had picked up his books and lunch, but was waiting to see that they made it all right.

By daylight, the other boy looked thin and pale. He was doing some talking, making it sound as though it had all been his idea for Beaver to crawl up on his back and get out of the hole.

"That was good thinking, Kit," the man said. Then he held out his hand to Beaver. "I'm Robert Markley. This is my son Christopher. I want to thank you for being so much help in what might have been a serious accident."

"I'm Theodore Cleaver," Beaver told him. "Most times, though, people call me Beaver."

He realized this must be the Mr. Markley that Dad and Mom had talked about, the one who owned the big house nearby and all of the hollow as well.

"Beaver Cleaver. It must be nice to have a name that rhymes," Mr. Markley said, smiling. Then, studying Beaver closely, he said, "Why, you must be the son of Ward and June Cleaver!"

"Yes, sir," Beaver said. "I've got a brother, too. His name is Wally. He's older than me."

Mr. Markley said, "I knew your parents a long time ago, about the time I was digging the mine here. Those were wonderful times. I was trying to relive them, taking the boards away and having a look into it."

Beaver thought it was sort of strange that a grown-up should want to look into an old hole, but he did not say so. His folks had always told him to be very polite when he was talking to grown-ups.

"We have just returned here to live," Mr. Markley continued, "and Kit doesn't know any-one in town yet. I hope you and he will be great friends, Beaver."

"Yes, sir," Beaver said, though he had some doubts about that. And he added, "I'm almost late for school now, so I've got to go. G'bye."

He was quite a bit late instead of almost. But the classroom door was open this warm spring day, and Miss Landers the teacher had her back turned, writing something on the board. He slipped inside and made it to his desk with the thought that maybe she wouldn't notice.

Whitey Whitney and Richard Rickover, a couple of his close friends, grinned and winked at him. Nobody said anything—but then, as Miss Landers turned to face the class again, Aggie Moss raised her hand and stood up.

"Miss Landers, Beaver Cleaver just sneaked in. He's late," Aggie Moss said, in her thin, twangy voice.

Beaver glared at her. She was a skinny girl who always wore old dresses, with her brown hair in pigtails, and she was constantly tattling on people, mostly on him.

Miss Landers bit her lip. "I was aware of his arrival, Agnes," she said. "Theodore, you will stay after school."

"Yes'm," Beaver said resignedly.

Miss Landers turned to the blackboard again. Aggie Moss made a face at Beaver, sticking out her tongue.

He glared again, but didn't do any more than that. His mother had told him he must always be polite to girls, too. Most of the time it wasn't difficult, because he could just pretend they didn't even exist. He couldn't do that with Aggie Moss, though. She was always causing some kind of trouble for him.

This day at school was about like any other. Beaver was studying hard and making pretty good grades, because his father was constantly telling him it wasn't too early to start getting ready for college. He didn't mind school too much.

Noon came after a while, and he ate his lunch with Whitey and Richard and a couple of other friends. They tried to figure out something to do to Aggie Moss that would stop her from tattling so much, but couldn't seem to think of anything, mostly because of the fact she could fight better than any boy in the class. She had proved it a couple of times, and it just didn't seem very smart to get her riled up.

After lunch they played softball during recreation time. Aggie Moss did the pitching. She could do that better than any boy, too.

Then, at length, the closing bell rang, and Beaver had to stay when the others filed out. Miss Landers told him he must write fifty times, "I am sorry I was tardy this morning." She waited at her desk while he did it, writing as fast as he could.

When he took the paper to her desk, Miss Landers said, "Theodore, I have a feeling you are thinking that it wasn't very nice of Agnes to report you this morning."

"Well—" Beaver said.

He was thinking it had been pretty doggoned

mean of Aggie, but didn't know what Miss Landers' reaction would be if he said so, and thus decided to keep it to himself.

"It wasn't nice," Miss Landers said. "But I would like to tell you something about Agnes. Things are very hard for her. She has a younger brother and sister to look after, for they don't have a mother, and her father is having difficulty finding work. There are days when I'm afraid they don't have enough to eat, though Agnes won't admit it. Will you remember that, Theodore, and make allowances for her when she seems to be unusually difficult?"

It was hard for Beaver to think of anybody not having enough to eat. This had certainly never happened to him.

"All right, Miss Landers," he agreed. "If you say so, it's what I'll try to do."

"Thank you," she said, smiling. "I knew I could count on you."

He went home then.

Mom was baking a cake in the kitchen, and

Eddie Haskell was there. He was saying, "I hope you are feeling well today, Mrs. Cleaver?"

"Yes, Eddie," Mom replied. "I am feeling quite well, thank you."

"And Mr. Cleaver?" Eddie said. "I trust he is feeling well, also?"

"As far as I know, Mr. Cleaver is enjoying quite good health," Mom said. "Why don't you go out and join Wally and Clarence Rutherford? They are in the side yard."

"Thank you," Eddie said. "I believe I will do that."

Eddie Haskell was a slim boy about Wally's age. He had curly fair hair. Mom had said he made her jittery. "It isn't normal for a boy to be that polite," she had told Ward Cleaver. "He makes me feel as though I'm a little old lady with a shawl about my shoulders."

Ward Cleaver had said, "I just wish some of his manners would rub off on Wally and Beaver."

June Cleaver greeted her younger son. "There is gingerbread in the cupboard, Beaver. Did you have a nice day at school?"

"I s'pose so," Beaver replied. He grabbed a hunk of gingerbread and headed out to the side yard, also.

Wally's other pal was there. Beaver spoke to him. "Hi, Lumpy."

"Listen, squirt, I've told you a hundred times to call me by my right name!" Lumpy Rutherford said.

"Okay, Lum—Clarence," Beaver said. He was called Lumpy because that was the way he looked, big and kind of awkward. He was bigger than either Eddie or Wally.

Wally was excited. "Listen, Eddie, Lumpy says he spotted a heap sitting back of Grimsby's garage, and that it's real keen. How about all of us going over there and taking a look at it?"

"Why not?" Eddie agreed. "Let's ambulate, men."

The three of them headed toward the street. Beaver tagged along. Lumpy stopped and looked around at him, frowning. "For gosh sake, Wally, has he got to come, too?"

"Beat it, Beave," Wally said.

Beaver didn't pay any attention. He could tell that Wally didn't really care if he went with them.

Grimsby's garage wasn't far away. The car was out in back. Wally said, "Hey, you're right, Lumpy! That's the best heap I ever saw!"

Beaver looked it over. It was an old car that didn't have any top and that was sort of battered here and there, with a lot of dents and scratches. He said, "It looks like a pile of junk to me."

"Who asked you, squirt?" Lumpy Rutherford said.

Mr. Grimsby's son came out of the garage. He was about sixteen, was pretty fat, and wore thick glasses. His name was Sylvester.

"Hey, what are you guys up to?" he demanded.

"Ah, we're just looking around," Wally replied. "Listen, Syl, what does your dad want for this heap?"

"Gosh, I don't know. Maybe a hundred bucks," Sylvester Grimsby replied. "He was saying that he got stuck with it and would go for about any deal if somebody would just take it off his hands."

"A hundred bucks? Boy!" Wally said. "I sure wish I could raise that much! Can we start the motor, Syl?"

"I guess so. The key is in it," Sylvester replied. "But you can't do any driving. None of you guys has even got a learner's permit yet."

"Look who's talking! Neither have you," Eddie said.

"I've done a lot of driving, though," Sylvester bragged. "I'm a pretty good driver."

The door by the wheel was standing open. In fact, Beaver noticed, it was almost falling off. Wally slid in and twisted the key. The motor coughed hard half a dozen times. A lot of blue smoke came out at the rear. Then the motor began to run, wheezing and gasping.

"Hey, look at me!" Wally cried, jiggling the wheel. "I'll bet I could really make this heap go!"

Beaver, who had never seen him so excited about anything, sniffed and said, "It sounds like an old broke-down cement mixer."

Nobody paid any attention to him. Eddie asked, "How about taking a look at that motor, men?"

Eddie went around in front to shove up the hood. It stuck, and Lumpy had to help him before it went up. Then they put their heads under the hood and began shouting at each other about spark plugs and distributors. Wally climbed out, leaving the motor running, and started to join them, but paused to kick at a tire.

Beaver scrambled into the front seat and took hold of the wheel. He jiggled it and felt a little excited, too.

Then he wondered if the car had a horn, and pushed a button in the middle of the wheel.

Beaver found out there was a horn, all right, about the loudest he had ever heard. Eddie and Lumpy found out, too. They yelled frantically and jerked their heads up, banging them hard against the underside of the hood.

The funny expressions on their faces made Beaver laugh for a moment. Then he stopped laughing, because the car was suddenly moving. It lurched forward, past Wally who was staring at Beaver with his mouth open, past Lumpy and Eddie and Sylvester Grimsby. The car began to pick up speed. It was heading straight toward a street where other cars were whizzing back and forth.

Beaver tried to remember what to do in order to stop a car, but couldn't. All he could do was grip the wheel desperately and hang on.

3
Trouble With Kit

What happened next seemed very surprising. There was a big pile of trash at one side of the garage. The car turned toward it, ran part way up the pile, then slid down again. It stopped all by itself.

The four boys behind Beaver were shouting at him. He twisted around, discovering he had come quite a distance. Then he saw those four running toward him, and decided that he had better get away from there.

It was not only that he didn't want to be in the car if it should start moving again. The looks on the faces of Eddie Haskell and Lumpy Rutherford and Sylvester Grimsby made him realize it was probably a very good idea to go somewhere else for a while.

Beaver could run pretty fast if he had to, and he ran fast now. He wasn't running from Wally, who stopped when he reached the car, or from Sylvester Grimsby, who couldn't run much anyway, being so fat, but from Eddie and Lumpy, who chased him for nearly a block before they gave up.

Beaver didn't know exactly why they were chasing him so hard, or why they shook their fists at him when they stopped. Eddie and Lumpy were only a few years older than himself, but some of the time Beaver didn't understand them any more than he understood grown-ups.

They were like Wally, who was always combing his hair and staring at himself in mirrors, and who had taken to hanging around a house near the high school. Wally didn't go into the house, he just sort of stood around outside, and Beaver had learned it wasn't wise to refer to the fact that a girl lived there.

Beaver went back home. Mom didn't seem to be in the house. He got another hunk of gingerbread, went out into the backyard, and found his red wagon.

Mom suddenly appeared as he was hauling the wagon toward the alley at the rear of the house. She said, "Are you going to play for a while, dear?"

"Gosh, no!" he said. Playing with a wagon was for little kids. He had told Mom that a number of times, but she didn't seem to remember. Sometimes it even seemed she thought he was still only a little kid himself. "I'm going to hunt for some bottles," Beaver said.

"That's nice," she said. "Don't stay out late."

It was the car which had made him think of hunting for bottles. Beaver didn't know why Wally got so excited over an old wreck of an automobile, but he had been reminded of the bicycle that he wanted so badly himself and had decided to start working for it right away.

Beaver stopped at the first trash box in the alley, where people threw out stuff they didn't want any longer. Right away he found two bottles that would be worth three cents each at the supermarket where Mom traded.

Grown-ups were sure strange, Beaver thought, throwing away valuable bottles. He tried to figure how many of them he would have to find before he could buy the bicycle.

He was about a block from home when all at once he saw Kit Markley again.

The other boy had changed his clothes. He was wearing a gray suit now, with a white shirt and bow tie. His shoes were freshly shined. He was eating ice cream on a stick and said, "Hi!"

"Listen," Beaver said, "why did you tell your father that it was your idea about us getting out of that old mine?"

"Well, I knew my mother would make a fuss when she heard about it, and give me something," Kit said. "Sure enough, she gave me a dollar."

Beaver stared at him. Just for falling down a hole this other boy had been handed as much as Beaver received for a whole week as his allowance.

Kit held out the ice-cream stick. "Here, you want a bite?" he asked.

"I don't guess so," Beaver said, and started on.

Kit went with him. "What are you doing?" he asked.

Beaver stared at him again. "My gosh, what does it look like I'm doing? I'm gathering bottles!" he said.

"Why?" Kit Markley demanded.

It came to Beaver then that the boy really didn't know why, so he explained.

Kit said, "If you want an old bicycle, why don't you ask your folks to give it to you? That's what I'd do."

Beaver snorted. He had a vivid mental image of asking his folks to give him the bicycle when it wasn't anywhere near either Christmas or his birthday. Besides, Ward Cleaver had strong ideas about boys working for and earning the things they wanted.

"I'll see you sometime," he said, and started on his way.

Kit Markley accompanied him. "I'll help you," he offered.

Beaver wasn't sure he wanted the other boy along. He wasn't even sure that he liked Kit Markley very much after what had happened at the mine.

But maybe with both of them working they could find more bottles. "Okay," Beaver said. "We'll go half on all we pick up from now on. You take that side of the alley, and I'll take this side."

Kit went away. He came back a couple of minutes later with an armful of bottles—milk bottles, vinegar bottles, and a catsup bottle which he was holding upside down. There had still been some catsup in it which had spilled all over his shirt.

Beaver felt a little exasperated with him. "Those aren't worth anything!" he said.

He tried to explain about the bottles that were worth something. Kit nodded and went away again. This time he brought back a bottle that was worth a cent, and three or four more of the worthless kind, including one that had spilled some black stuff, maybe medicine, on top of the catsup.

They worked on along the alley, and things happened to Kit Markley.

He tried to climb a fence, and got his jacket caught on something, tearing it.

Then he went into the yard of some people named Considine who had a big dog which barked fiercely, though he hardly ever bit anybody. The dog chased Kit all over the yard and he finally fell down in a place which Mrs. Considine had soaked good for a flower bed.

Beaver calmed the dog down, then borrowed the Considine hose and managed to wash some of the mud off Kit. He tried to wash the catsup and black stuff off, too, but didn't have much luck doing that.

"Look," he told Kit, "you just pull the wagon for a while, and I'll look for the bottles."

A little later they encountered a girl who also

was collecting bottles. She was pulling along a box by a rope that was tied to it, with a ragged, dirty little boy helping her. Beaver felt surprised, because he had never before known a girl to do such a thing. Then he realized the girl was Aggie Moss.

She reacted instantly at the sight of him. "You clear out of here, Beaver Cleaver!" Aggie yelled. "I've got first dibs on the bottles in this alley!"

"What are you talking about?" Beaver demanded. "Nobody ever has first dibs on bottles!"

Aggie did not waste time arguing. She grabbed up a rock and threw it. The rock missed Beaver, but it plunked Kit Markley in the ribs. Kit yelped and backed off.

Beaver decided to retreat, also. It was growing late, for one thing, and he also knew his mother wouldn't like it at all if he threw rocks at a girl, even though she had thrown at him first.

"I guess we've got enough bottles for this time," he told Kit. "We'll go and collect on them."

"That's sure a mean girl," Kit grumbled. "We

ought to chase her away, or something."

But he went with Beaver, because Aggie Moss had picked up several more rocks and was ready to use them. Kit added, "Who is she?"

"Oh, just a girl I know in school," Beaver replied. This reminded him of something. He went on, "Say, where do you go to school?"

"I don't," Kit answered. "I have a tutor."

Beaver knew what a tutor was. It was the same as if Miss Landers were to spend her whole time teaching only Beaver Cleaver at his home. He didn't think he would like that. School was more fun, even with Aggie Moss around to pester him.

They arrived at the supermarket where a clerk checked the bottles and gave Beaver thirty-five cents. Then he stared at Kit Markley and laughed. "Hey, kid," he said, "you must have had a fight in a paint store!"

Kit looked sort of strange, all right. Some mud had gotten into his hair which was standing straight up. His shirt was all red and black and his suit was now more yellow than gray from dried mud. His shoes were no longer shiny. Also, he had torn his jacket again. Beaver didn't know when that had happened.

Outside, Beaver handed him ten cents. "This is your share," he said. It was really more than Kit had coming, but maybe he deserved a little extra for trying hard.

"So long," Beaver said. "Maybe I'll see you again some time."

He left, then, with Kit just standing there, still holding the dime and looking after him.

When Beaver got home, neither his father nor Wally had arrived yet. His mother was fixing supper. "Don't you wander away, now," she told him.

"I won't," Beaver promised.

He went out and sat down on the front porch, thinking about the quarter he had made during the afternoon. If he could only make that much every day, it wouldn't be any time at all until he could buy the bicycle.

The trouble was, he didn't think he could make

a quarter every day. Grown-ups didn't throw that many bottles away. Besides, Aggie Moss was hunting for them, too.

Beaver wondered again why a girl was collecting bottles. Then he forgot about Aggie Moss, for a big, long black car coming along the street suddenly stopped in front of the Cleaver house. A man was driving. He wore a uniform and cap.

The man opened the rear door of the car. A lady got out. She had Kit Markley with her. Kit looked the same as when Beaver had left him at the supermarket. He was rubbing his eyes and sniffing.

"That's the one, Mama!" he said, pointing at Beaver.

"You wicked boy!" the lady cried.

Beaver said, "Who, me?"

He couldn't understand why she was so upset.

Beaver's mother came through the front door. "What on earth—?" she began. Then she stared at the angry lady. "Why, Enid Markley!" she said in a surprised tone.

The lady stared back at her. "June—?" she said.

"How nice to see you again," June Cleaver remarked.

The lady didn't seem to think it was nice. "Is this your son?" she demanded, pointing at Beaver. "Well, I want you to take a look at what he did to my Christopher! Take a good look!"

"But I didn't do it!" Beaver protested.

Saying that didn't help him any, though. It never did, when a grown-up was yelling at him. Mrs. Markley was sort of slender and wore expensive-looking clothes. She was good-looking, though not nearly as good-looking as Mom. And she was angrier than any lady Beaver had ever seen.

June Cleaver said, after a bit, "Go to your room, Beaver."

"Aw, gee, Mom!" he protested.

"Theodore, go to your room," his mother told him.

When she called him by his right name, Mom

LEAVE IT TO BEAVER   51

meant business. Beaver went inside, dragging his feet, and headed upstairs.

He knew what would happen from now on. When his father got home, Mom would talk it over with him, and then Beaver would be summoned downstairs to the den.

He didn't like having to face his father in the den. It would mean punishment of some kind. And while it was bad enough to be punished for something he had done, it was even worse when he wasn't at fault.

"Doggone that Kit Markley!" Beaver said, kicking at a stair step. "He sure had better not come near me again!"

It did not seem likely anything like that was going to happen, considering how much trouble the boy had caused for him, Beaver thought. He was wrong, though. He was going to see more of Kit Markley, and get in more trouble because of him.

It was going to happen before very long, too.

4
A Car
of His Own

Wally came in presently. "Gee, Beave, it looks like you're in trouble with just about everybody!"

Beaver was sitting on his bed trying to read some comic books. Wally went on, "You made Eddie and Lumpy nearly deaf, sounding that horn when they had their heads under the hood."

"I—I didn't mean to," Beaver said.

"I told them that. Lumpy said he was going to give you a good swat. I told him he had better not, or I'd see to it that he really had some lumps," Wally said.

There were times, Beaver thought, when it was pretty nice to have an older brother. "Thanks, Wally," he said.

"Well, somebody has to stand up for you, the kookie things that you do sometimes," Wally told him, going to look at himself in a mirror.

Beaver thought about this for a moment. "Wally, what does kookie mean?" he asked.

"It's a word for somebody that acts kind of weird," Wally replied.

"I don't mean to act weird," Beaver said. "I didn't mean to make Mr. Grimsby's car run."

"I guess you didn't, at that," Wally said. "It must have started all by itself, some way. You handled it good, though, not running into anything and turning the wheel so it would stop against the trash pile."

Beaver was quite surprised. "Did I do that?"

"You must have. It could have started by itself, but it couldn't turn unless you turned the wheel."

Beaver found this very exciting. "I drove an automobile, all by myself!" he exclaimed.

Thinking about such an accomplishment made him feel a little better.

Wally combed his hair. Then he sat down at

his desk and started to do some figuring.

Beaver had heard voices from below for a while —Mrs. Markley's voice mostly, sounding as though she was still angry. It was quiet now. Dad was probably home, he thought, and Mom was conferring with him in the den. Before long, Beaver would be summoned there. Dad would be very stern, which was as bad as the punishment that would be handed out—no movies or TV for a while, plus special jobs to do, and likely a loss of part of his allowance.

It didn't happen, though. Instead, Mom tapped on the door, calling, "Wash up, boys. Dinner is ready." And when Beaver went downstairs, he saw that Mrs. Markley and Kit were gone, but Mr. Markley was talking to Dad in the lower hall.

Kit's father smiled at him, not acting angry at all. He said, "Hello again, Beaver."

Mom and Dad went with Mr. Markley to the front door, where he said, "Ward and June, you don't know how good it is to see you once more after so many years!"

He left. Ward Cleaver looked after him. Presently he said, "I can't get over it. All Bob could talk about was a dime his son made collecting bottles this afternoon with Beaver. It is the first money the boy has ever earned in his whole life. Bob was as pleased as punch."

"I don't think Kit meant to put the blame on Beaver," June Cleaver said. "Enid Markley was so angry and upset that he was afraid to say anything else. She was very apologetic when the truth finally came out that it wasn't Beaver's fault."

"Bob apologized, also," Ward Cleaver said.

Beaver heard his mother giggle. "I know it's awful of me to laugh, but I can't help it," she said. "That boy looked like a scarecrow!"

Dad chuckled. "He certainly did—reminded me of the time when I fell on my face in some wet cement!"

They turned and started toward the dining room where Wally was waiting. But Beaver's father put a hand on his arm. "I want a word with you, Beaver," he said.

It seemed that maybe there was going to be some punishment after all. However, Dad went on talking, and it came out that Mr. Markley had talked to him about Kit and Beaver being friends. Also, Beaver discovered in dismay that his father thought this was a good idea.

"Aw, gee, Dad!" he protested. "I don't want to have anything more to do with him. He—he's kookie!"

"You mean, he's a drip?" his father asked. "That's what I would have called him, I suppose, when I was your age."

"You would have?" Beaver said. It was always a little difficult for Beaver to realize that his father had once been as young as Beaver was now.

"I suppose that Kit is—er—kookie," Dad continued. "But it isn't really his fault, Beaver."

He went on to explain that the Markleys had lived in a lot of different big cities, mostly in hotels. Kit not only had never gone to school, he had never had any friends at all.

"I feel that is rather sad," Ward Cleaver said. "Don't you, son?"

Beaver tried to think what it would be like if there was no school for him, if he didn't have friends like Whitey and Richard and a lot of others. "I guess so," he agreed.

The Markleys were back, living in the big house at the hollow, and Kit's father was worried about his son, who had missed so much that went with growing up.

Beaver's father said, "Bob Markley was a good friend of mine once. I would like to see his boy get a break. You would be doing me a favor if you gave him a chance, Beaver."

It was like Dad to put it that way, Beaver thought. He wasn't much for ordering his sons to do something, but instead pointed out what he thought was the right thing to do, then left it up to them.

"All right," Beaver decided. "I'll give him a chance."

Dad squeezed his shoulder. "Good!"

They went on into the dining room, where Wally said, "Can we eat now? I'm just about starved!"

"You are?" his father said, sitting down. "I suppose it must be your weak, emaciated state, then, that kept you from mowing the back lawn this afternoon, when we agreed the grass was so high there that somebody was liable to get lost in it if it wasn't cut at once."

"Gosh, Dad, I forgot," Wally said. "I'll do it right after school tomorrow. Honest!"

"Let us hope so," Dad said. "Otherwise, I am liable to grow slightly forgetful myself, along about Friday."

Since Friday was the day when Dad gave them their allowances, Beaver thought it was pretty likely that Wally would be very busy about three o'clock tomorrow.

Dinner was meat loaf, fixed the way only Mom could cook it, and mashed potatoes, corn on the cob and spinach, with banana cake for dessert.

Beaver tried to skip the spinach, but his mother saw to it that he didn't. When he finally folded the napkin and said, " 'Scuse me, please," it was with a feeling that he didn't want anything more to eat for quite a while—not until a light snack just before bedtime, anyway.

His father, sipping a second cup of coffee, remarked, "Wally, from the amount of food you put away, I almost believe you meant it when you said you were starved."

"I didn't eat so much, Dad!" Wally protested. "Only the food with proteins in it—and no cake. I'm in training."

"I think you must be training for the fat men's race at the Sunday school picnic next summer," Ward Cleaver said.

"Now, Ward, stop it," June Cleaver said, "or I'll tell them about the time when you ate a whole watermelon down on your uncle's farm when you were a boy."

"Gee, Dad, you didn't! You couldn't!" Beaver exclaimed.

"He had a king-sized tummy-ache, too," Mom said.

Dad made a face at Mom, and then laughed. "Boys, never marry a girl whom you have known since she had pigtails and freckles," he said. "Your mother remembers too much about me, and tells only the things that sound funny. She doesn't tell you about—well, for instance, the time I was lost in the woods for three days on a hiking trip, with nothing to eat."

"You must have been mighty hungry!" Wally said.

"It should happen to you—not getting lost, but knowing what it means really to be hungry," Dad said.

Beaver found he was remembering that Miss Landers had said Aggie Moss had to go hungry at times. He wondered whether she was hungry tonight. Then he forgot about her, helping to clear the table off, and drying while Wally washed. Next week, they would switch jobs.

Afterward, he started upstairs to get at his

homework which had to be finished before he could watch TV. He remembered he had put his books on a chair outside of the den when he came home, so he went to get them.

Wally and Dad were talking in the den. Beaver didn't eavesdrop, exactly, but he did take his time picking up the books and couldn't help hearing them.

"—so maybe we can buy this heap from Mr. Grimsby for a hundred bucks," Wally was saying eagerly. "Lumpy and Eddie think they can raise twenty-five bucks apiece. If I can get hold of the rest, we'll buy it as partners!"

"It doesn't sound like a very equal sort of partnership," Dad said drily. "Also, if I know Eddie —and I do know Eddie—he would somehow manage to get possession of the car before very long so that you and Lumpy probably would never see it again."

"No, sir!" Wally said. "I told Eddie plain, it is going to stay right here at our place!"

"I don't know where you would put it," Dad

said. "I am not in favor of having the family car evicted from our garage, and I don't think the neighbors would care to have your—er—heap in either the driveway or at the curb."

"I'll put it in the alley!" Wally said.

"Son, I don't want to throw cold water on your plans," Dad said, "but we had better look at some hard facts. To begin with, you couldn't drive the car even if you somehow managed to buy it."

"But, Dad, it won't be any time at all before I can apply for a learner's permit!" Wally protested.

· "True. But you will then have to wait a year before you can get an operator's license which will allow you to drive any car alone," Dad pointed out.

"Well, I could just work on the heap and fix it up good until I did get an operator's license," Wally said.

"That would be like giving Beaver an exciting toy on Christmas morning and telling him he couldn't play with it," Dad told him. "You simply

couldn't have a car and resist the temptation of driving it. No, Wally, I'm afraid I can't agree to any such proposal."

"Please, Dad—" Wally said.

"The subject is closed, son."

This meant Wally wasn't to say anything more about it. But Wally had something more to say, anyway. "If I can—well, earn fifty dollars some way, on my own, will you let me talk to you about it again?" he asked.

"Why, yes, in that event I think the subject can be reopened," Dad replied, sounding as though he wasn't much worried that Wally would find a way to come up with fifty dollars.

Wally went out through the den's other door. After a moment Mom spoke. She was in the den, also. "Ward, weren't you a little hard on him?" Mom asked.

"I don't think so," Dad replied. "Facts are facts, June. They have to be faced."

"I am remembering your first car," Mom said. "You were only about a year older than Wally is now when you bought it. And you took me for a ride before you had a driver's license. Don't you remember, Ward?"

"I got a license pretty soon afterward, though," Dad said. "Also, I think the conditions were different. I was more responsible than Wally is, and older for my years. I had worked two summers on my uncle's farm, pitching hay, to earn that car. I had learned the value of a dollar the hard way, which Wally hasn't done yet."

"You were pretty lucky to have an uncle who owned a farm," Mom said. "He doesn't own it any longer, so Wally won't have the same chance that you did to earn money and become responsible. But I have a feeling he will find a way to earn his fifty dollars, and you had better be thinking of what to say to him when he comes to talk to you about it again!"

"Hmm!" Dad said, still sounding as though he wasn't much worried that any such thing was likely to happen. Then he laughed. "Say, I had completely forgotten about that first jalopy of mine! We had some pretty good times with it, didn't we?"

"That isn't all you have forgotten," Mom said. "I may have had pigtails but I didn't have freckles, and don't you ever tell anybody else that I did!"

They both laughed together, and started talking about the vacation trip that all of them were going to take in the mountains in July. Beaver decided it was time to get upstairs and do his homework.

5
False Alarm!

Wally was in their room and doing some figuring when Beaver got there.

"Maybe I can sell my stamp collection for about ten bucks," Wally said. "Then, maybe I can find somebody to buy that short-wave radio I built once for another ten bucks. But doggone it, I would still need a lot of money."

Beaver said, "I saw an ad in a magazine that said you could send away for stuff and sell it, and keep half of what you make."

"I tried that once, when I was about as old as you are now," Wally said. "A company sent me some packages of dye, but I could only sell three of them. Mom bought one, and so did Dad."

"Who bought the third one?" Beaver asked.

"Well, Mom did, after nobody else would," Wally said. "Then Dad made me send all of the rest back."

He did more figuring. "I've got to get hold of the money some way—and so do Eddie and Lumpy. If we don't, Mr. Grimsby is liable to sell the heap to somebody else."

Beaver knew how he felt. It was the same fear he had concerning the bicycle, that somebody would buy it from Mr. Hallam before he had a chance to do so.

Nevertheless, he said, "Listen, Wally, I made a quarter today collecting bottles. You can have it."

"Thanks, Beave, but a quarter wouldn't help very much," Wally said. "You keep it."

He kept on figuring and muttering to himself all evening. Wally didn't go down after a while to watch TV, even though there was a good western on. He didn't even look at himself in the mirror at bedtime to see whether he had to shave.

Next day at school nothing much happened, except that Aggie Moss confronted Beaver in the hall at noon and told him to stop collecting bottles. "I've got first dibs," she said. "And if you don't stop I'll make you real sorry, Beaver Cleaver!"

"Ah, you're a mean old girl and you can't stop me from doing anything!" Beaver said. But he didn't say it until after she had walked away from him.

Doggone girls anyway, he told himself. They could do just about anything and a boy had to take it because there were always people around, like Miss Landers and Mom, to make sure he did.

He still couldn't understand why Aggie had to act so mean over a few bottles.

After school, when he got home, Wally hadn't shown up yet. But Kit Markley was out front waiting.

Kit was wearing still another suit today, a blue one with a necktie and with his shoes shined again. Looking him over, Beaver said, "You sure must have a lot of clothes."

He seemed to dress up every day the way Beaver did only on Sunday or for something special, like when relatives came for dinner. Kit bragged, "I have ten suits and all of the accessories for formal occasions."

" 'Cessories? What are they?" Beaver asked.

"Why, gloves and hats and handkerchiefs," Kit said. "My mother says I must be well turned out."

Beaver had a suit and next-best suit, but spent as much time as he could in blue jeans and a jacket.

He carried a handkerchief—had to, because Mom was always checking—in his hip pocket, but he didn't own a hat or gloves, and would crawl under the house and hide before he would ever appear in public with either. The kids at school would never let him forget it if he did.

"Well, if you get messed up today, don't go telling your folks it was my fault!" Beaver warned.

"I won't," Kit promised. "What are we going to do?"

Beaver didn't know. They went in the house

because he had to dispose of his books. Mom was there. She said, "Why, hello, Christopher."

"Good afternoon, Mrs. Cleaver," Kit said. "How are you today? Well, I trust?"

"Oh, no!" Mom said. "Not another Eddie!"

Beaver had to put his hand over his mouth to keep from laughing. He knew what Mom was thinking, that another boy as polite as Eddie was almost too much to take.

"I beg your pardon, Mrs. Cleaver?" Kit said.

"Never mind," Mom told him. "You two run along. If you are back about four, I'll have some fresh-baked cookies."

Beaver decided to go look at the bicycle, and to take Kit with him. On the way he told all about it, but with a feeling that he couldn't describe how beautiful the bike really was.

It stood in the show window of the small shop where Mr. Hallam repaired bicycles and washing machines and just about everything else. There was a sign: SPECIAL—FOR SALE—$21.00.

Somebody had owned the English bike but

didn't want it any longer and had turned it over to Mr. Hallam to sell if he could. Beaver couldn't understand anybody owning such a bicycle and not wanting it any longer.

"The tires are nearly new, and it's got front and back fenders, gears for three speeds, hand brakes for both wheels, and a spotlight and taillight, with tools to fix anything that goes wrong!" he told Kit.

"I can see all those things for myself," Kit said. "It's kind of worn, though. There are places where there isn't any paint."

"I'll paint it all over, just like new!" Beaver said.

Mr. Hallam came out of his shop and said hello. He was thin and old, like Captain Gus, but very brisk and businesslike. Beaver introduced Kit, who shook hands and was polite to him. Then Mr. Hallam said, "Are you still interested in the bicycle, Beaver? If so, you mustn't delay too long. Several other parties have inquired about it, and if anyone offers me the twenty-one dollars I'm afraid that I'll have to accept it."

Beaver's heart seemed to stop for a moment on hearing this. "I-I'm going to do my best to make the money and buy it, Mr. Hallam," he said.

"I hope you can. I would like to see you have the bike, but its owner insists that I sell it as soon as possible," Mr. Hallam said, and went back into his shop.

Beaver continued to look at the bicycle through the show window. He had been allowed to ride it once, and itched to do so again, but was afraid to ask for fear Mr. Hallam would think he was a nuisance.

He was a pretty good rider. Wally had had a bike, and had passed it on to Beaver, who had used it for a while until it was just sort of worn out. But it hadn't been anything like this bicycle.

Maybe, Beaver thought, Mr. Hallam wouldn't mind if Kit tried it out. He suggested this, but Kit shook his head. "And let's do something else," the other boy said. "Just standing around here isn't any fun."

"Okay," Beaver agreed reluctantly. "We'll go

to the fire station. You can meet Captain Gus and General."

On the way to the fire station he talked about his need to raise enough money so he could buy the bicycle.

"Well, you can't raise very much by collecting bottles, like you were doing yesterday," Kit said. "There aren't enough of them around—and anyway, there's that mean girl who is also looking for them."

"I s'pose you're right," Beaver admitted. "I'll have to figure out something else."

"I can't understand why you don't just ask your folks for it," Kit said. "That's what I would do. I'd go to them and say, 'There's an old bicycle at Hallam's place that I want.' And they'd get it for me."

"Would they get you anything you might ask for?" Beaver inquired.

"Sure! Oh, sometimes my father fusses a little and says it seems like I've got too much already, but if I keep asking he usually gives in. Or I just go to my mother and she gets it for me right away."

Beaver thought for a moment of how things might be if his folks were like Kit Markley's folks. It would be Christmas nearly every day, he supposed.

He was surprised to discover that he didn't think he would care for that very much. Christmas was fine, of course, but most of the fun was looking forward to it and remembering how it had been, with the satisfaction of giving presents as well as receiving them. Just to be given things all the time would get pretty tiresome, Beaver thought.

"Sometimes I don't even have to ask my mother," Kit went on. "If I only say I saw something I like, she is liable to go right down and buy it for me."

Beaver wondered if Kit had ever given his mother anything, the way he did himself at Christmas, on Mom's birthday and on Mother's Day, after planning and saving from his allowance and going without stuff for himself.

It didn't seem very likely Kit had ever done that. All at once Beaver felt sorry for him.

They reached the fire station to discover Captain Gus had stepped out for a couple of minutes. But General was there to sniff at Kit's hand and wave his tail and let his head be patted, indicating he was willing to accept Kit, providing he behaved himself.

The fireman on duty at the desk in Captain Gus's place said it was all right for them to look around, if they didn't fool with anything. So Beaver showed Kit the pole that the firemen slid down from where they slept upstairs, and their boots and helmets, all arranged so they could be put on in a hurry.

They inspected the big pumper truck with General jumping up on the seat to show where he rode.

"Shucks, this isn't such a big truck," Kit said. "I used to see a hook-and-ladder truck in San Francisco that was at least a hundred feet long, with a man on the back end to steer it around corners."

"I'll bet it doesn't get to fires as fast as this one does!" Beaver said.

"I'll bet it does!" Kit said.

They stood around for a while arguing and hoping maybe there would be a fire, but nothing happened. General left them, curled up under Captain Gus's desk and dozed. Captain Gus claimed he could count the taps on the alarm gong and was always the first one to reach the truck when it was supposed to roll.

"This isn't any fun, either," Kit said at last. "Let's go do something else."

They started back toward the Cleaver house. Beaver wanted to talk again about the bicycle, but Kit was still interested in the fire station. He asked how the firemen found out when there was a fire, and also where they should go.

"I thought everybody knew that!" Beaver said. But it was obvious Kit didn't know, so he explained that people either called in by phone or else turned in the signal at an alarm box.

Then he had to hunt for a box to show what he meant, and found one about four blocks from the fire station. Because it was also obvious Kit had never seen one before, Beaver told him how an iron bolt hanging on a chain was used to smash a little glass window, and how you then reached inside to turn a knob.

"Right away, there is a signal at fire head-quarters downtown," Beaver said, "and the gong sounds at Captain Gus's fire station, saying the alarm was turned in at this box. So the truck comes here. It does that real fast, too, with sirens and bells and everything!"

Kit laughed. "Well, what are we waiting for?" he said. "Let's find out right now just how fast they are!"

Then, to Beaver's horror and before he could do anything to stop Kit, the boy broke the glass with the iron bolt, reached inside and turned the knob.

Beaver gasped. He couldn't speak for a few

moments. He couldn't even breathe.

Off in the distance, the moaning wail of a siren began. Kit Markley giggled. "We're going to see everything real good, the same as if there was a real fire!" he said.

Beaver found his voice. "You just turned in a false alarm!" he cried. "That's against the law! They can put you in jail for doing such a thing!"

Kit's eyes grew big and round. His mouth trembled. He began to back away. "No!" he said hoarsely. "They can't! My-my father and mother won't let them!"

The boy turned and ran. He raced across a vacant lot and around the corner of a house, out of sight.

The siren was growing louder and the bells were clanging as the fire truck thundered toward Beaver, with its big red blinker light working. Then it braked to a stop right beside him.

All of the firemen looked at the alarm box, with its broken glass, then at Beaver. Captain Gus slid down from the front seat, staring at him in astonishment and dismay.

"Beaver, I—I don't understand this at all," he said unsteadily. "What does it mean?"

Beaver gulped hard, realizing there wasn't anything he could say in reply to Captain Gus, who had been such a good friend to him—just not anything at all.

6
Beaver's Big Job

After a few minutes the truck returned to the fire station, with Beaver riding between Captain Gus and General. He was afraid that neither of them would ever want to be friends with him again.

Captain Gus had said, "Beaver, I have to know who it was that broke the glass and turned in the alarm here."

Beaver had stood silent before him, feeling worse than he ever had in his whole life.

Captain Gus had sighed, then, looking sadly at Beaver. "I didn't think a time would come when you wouldn't want to talk to me," he had said. "I guess you had better ride back with us while

I try to figure out what to do."

Beaver had always wanted to ride the big pumper truck, but not like this. It seemed that everybody they passed was looking at him and pointing, that all of them were saying he had turned in a false alarm.

When the truck reached the fire station, Captain Gus said, "Just sit down somewhere and wait, Beaver."

Captain Gus would call the police now, Beaver thought. Then they would come for him, and he would be taken to jail.

But the police didn't come for him. Instead, after a bit Mom suddenly appeared, hurrying into the fire station, and Dad was right behind her. It made things even worse to realize that Dad had had to leave his office and come here, on account of what had happened.

Mom patted Beaver's shoulder, but didn't say anything. Then she and Dad and Captain Gus talked together, their voices low, all of them looking toward Beaver occasionally.

General suddenly came and put his head in Beaver's lap, soft eyes liquid and sympathetic. This made him feel a little bit better.

Beaver remembered how he had felt sorry for Kit Markley. Now he wished he could get his hands on him.

At last, Dad came to Beaver. "We're going home, son," he said. "And do you have anything to say now to Captain Gus?"

"Yes, sir," Beaver replied. "Captain Gus, I-I'm awfully sorry."

"So am I, Beaver." Captain Gus sighed. "So am I."

Beaver rode in the back seat of the Cleaver sedan on the drive home, with his parents in the front seat. He decided that it looked as though he wasn't going to be turned over to the police, but instead would be punished by his father.

He felt that he would almost prefer going to jail, rather than having to face his father in the den.

Nobody said anything until they were almost

there, when Mom broke the silence. "Ward, are you sure that what you are planning to do about all this is right?"

"No, I'm not sure, June," Dad replied. "But I mean to try it and hope for the best, anyway."

They went into the house together. It was still fairly early in the afternoon. Dad pointed to a chair by the stairs in the front hall. "Wait there, Beaver," he directed. "I have something to do, first. After that I'll talk to you."

Dad went into the den. Mom brought Beaver some cookies and a glass of milk. "Don't worry, dear," she said. "I'm certain that everything is going to work out fine."

Beaver wished he could be certain, too, as he ate the cookies and drank the milk.

Dad was on the phone in the den talking to somebody, then listening. He hung up, dialed again and spoke briefly to somebody else. At last he called, "Come in here, son."

Beaver walked into the den. He stopped by the desk that Dad used occasionally when he worked nights at home. Beaver braced himself. Dad had always said that you must stand by what you did, and take the consequences like a man.

Dad said, "I think I know why you wouldn't tell Captain Gus anything, but I'll ask you myself: who broke the glass at that signal box and turned in the alarm?"

Beaver bit his lip. He still couldn't say anything, not even to his father.

"I was just talking to Mr. Markley," Dad went on. "He said Kit came home in an almost hysterical state, but wouldn't say what caused it. You and Kit were here, and went away together, then were at the fire station just before the alarm was turned in. Were you still together when that happened?"

Words burst from Beaver, then: "Don't ask me any more, Dad! Please don't!"

His father relaxed a little, leaning back in his chair. "Captain Gus couldn't understand why you wouldn't tell him anything," he said. "But I guess it has been longer since Captain Gus was a boy than since I was, and he doesn't remember how wrong it is to snitch on somebody."

Beaver relaxed a little, also, glad that his father understood.

Dad—and Wally, too—had always said that almost the worst thing you could do was to snitch. This was the reason why Beaver had known from the time Kit Markley had started running that he would have to take the blame for the false alarm, because he just couldn't tattle on the other boy and tell that Kit had done it.

It didn't matter that Kit Markley was kookie. Beaver didn't ever want to see him again, but he was ready to take whatever punishment was necessary because of the false alarm, while still not snitching. He told his father this, and added, "Will I have to go to jail, now?"

Dad's lips twitched a little, as though he was almost smiling. "No, I don't think so," he replied. "However, there will have to be some punishment."

Beaver braced himself again. "Yes, sir," he said.

Dad went on, "Captain Gus said he couldn't believe you would ever turn in a false alarm by yourself—but he is afraid that you must have had something to do with it. He told me you have been at the fire station a great deal, and he feels you might have been—well, tempted to watch the pumper truck in action, then were so frightened afterwards that you couldn't talk about it."

Beaver almost cried out that it hadn't been that way at all. He managed, though, to keep silent.

"I am not saying I believe that," Dad continued. "I have my own idea about what happened, but I'll keep it to myself. Mr. Markley is going to apologize for whatever Kit might have done, and I have just apologized on your behalf to Captain Gus, who is willing to let it go at that and will not do anything more. I don't know what else Mr. Markley may do where Kit is concerned—"

Beaver almost sniffed. He had a strong hunch

nothing would be done to Kit.

"—but we Cleavers always stand by what we do, even when it is not snitching on somebody, and take the consequences," Dad said. "So as punishment you are not to go to the fire station again for a while—quite a while, I think."

It was hard to take, that he couldn't visit there and see General, but Beaver said, "I won't, Dad."

"Good," Dad said. "Now, with that out of the way, there's something else—"

He hesitated. All at once Beaver knew what was coming next, and cried, "Don't ask me to be friends any more with that Kit Markley! Please don't!"

Dad leaned farther back in his chair, and studied him thoughtfully. "Beaver, assuming that Kit turned in the alarm—though, mind you, I'm not saying he did—do you think he ought to go to jail?"

"Well—uh—no," Beaver replied.

"Why not?"

"I guess mostly because I wouldn't want such

a thing to happen to anybody," Beaver said. "But also because it wouldn't be fair. He didn't even know what a signal box was, or that it would be wrong for someone to turn in an alarm if there wasn't a fire—"

Beaver caught himself, realizing he had almost said too much.

"There are a lot of things you know that most boys learn just by growing up," Dad said. "But Kit doesn't know them. He found out something today, that it is wrong to turn in a false alarm. How is he going to find out all of the other things he ought to know? A lot of different persons showed you the right and wrong ways of doing things. Don't you think Kit ought to have someone who could start showing him?"

"I guess so," Beaver admitted reluctantly. "But why does it have to be me?"

Dad smiled. "I can't think of anybody who could do a better job!" he said.

Those words gave Beaver a warm, pleased feeling. Dad didn't often praise either him or

Wally, and when he did they knew he really meant it.

"Okay," Beaver said. "Kit Markley can come around some more if he wants to."

"I think that ends this session, then," Dad said, standing up. "And I must get back to the office and clean up the work I left there."

Beaver went through the house since the clatter of the mower on the rear lawn told him Wally was at work there.

Mom was in the kitchen starting dinner. She said, "Is everything all right?"

"I s'pose so," he replied. Then, after watching her for a minute, he went on, "Mom why did the Markleys live around a lot of places in hotels, so Kit never had a chance to make friends and find out about things?"

"Oh, dear! I'm not sure you will understand, but I'll try to explain, anyway," Mom said. "The Markleys have a great deal of money. They thought it was right that they should travel a lot, and have servants. Kit's parents now feel that that was a mistake. They are trying to settle down in the house at the hollow and live as normal a life as they can, for Kit's sake."

It sounded to Beaver as though Kit were being a lot of trouble for everybody.

Mom said, "Scoot, now. And we'll be eating dinner a little later than usual, since we'll have to wait for your father to come home again."

Beaver went on out, wondering if Kit Markley was worth the effort of trying to show him about things. Then he forgot the other boy, because Eddie and Lumpy were with Wally, and it immediately became evident that they had had no luck whatever in trying to raise the money to buy Mr. Grimsby's car.

Both of Wally's pals scowled at Beaver, but he ignored this, knowing Wally wouldn't let them try doing anything to him because he had sounded the horn.

Lumpy said, "When I asked my father if I could kind of borrow twenty-five bucks from him to go partners in buying the heap, he started yelling no and didn't stop even after I was clear out of the house."

"You were lucky that you could get out," Eddie said. "Mine started delivering his lecture about how I must think money grows on trees. I've heard it so many times I can say it by heart, but I had to stay there and hear the whole thing again anyway."

The two boys sat on the grass and watched Wally push the mower back and forth. He reported that he hadn't had any luck, either. Nobody had been interested in buying his stamp collection or his short-wave radio, at any price.

"I'm going to find some way to raise the money, though," Wally announced determinedly. "You guys just wait and see!"

"Well, you had better find a way for us to raise some, too," Eddie Haskell said. "Because if you don't, we won't be any better off than we are now."

"Hey, I've got an idea!" Lumpy said. "Mr. Grimsby might let us borrow the heap if we promise that we'll pay for it as soon as we can make some money—maybe during vacation."

"You've got rocks in your head!" Eddie said scornfully, standing up. "People don't let other people borrow cars—and especially if those other people are kids. And I'm tired of talking. I think I'll go home."

"How about waiting until I'm finished?" Wally said. "Then we can go take another look at the heap, anyway."

"You got us to go and take a look at it during noon hour today," Eddie said. "And Syl told me his father wanted to know what we were doing hanging around there so much. I don't think he likes it. So long, Wally. I'll see you later."

He started off, and Lumpy got up to leave, also. But Wally cried, "Wait a minute!"

Wally was suddenly very excited. "All of us have got rocks in our heads!" he said. "How do other people buy cars, mostly? They pay some money down, then some more every week, or month. I'll bet Mr. Grimsby would let us have the heap if we offered to give him a dollar down and a dollar a week, until it's all paid for!"

"Huh?" Lumpy said. "But we haven't got a dollar. All of us are broke—"

"Don't be so dense!" Eddie told him. Eddie had also become excited. "We all get allowances every week, don't we? And we could manage to save a dollar a week between us if we're real careful about spending and cut out some other things!"

"Sure, we could," Wally said. "Lumpy could almost save a dollar all by himself if he would just quit eating so many candy bars."

"Now, you listen!" Lumpy said angrily. "I don't eat so much!"

"Ah, forget it," Wally said. "Let's go talk to Mr. Grimsby right now. Then if we can only scrape up a dollar somewhere for a down payment, maybe we'll all be part owners of a car right away!"

Wally and Eddie started off, walking fast. Lumpy hesitated a moment, then hurried after them. And Beaver trailed along behind. He had to see what happened next.

7
Bad News
for Wally

At first, Beaver was almost as excited as Wally over the possibility of buying the car at Grimsby's for so much down and so much a week, because if the plan worked maybe Mr. Hallam would let him have the bicycle on a similar deal.

Before long, though, Beaver found himself thinking of some facts that it seemed Wally, in his enthusiasm, had overlooked.

Neither he nor Wally ever had any extra money to speak of, because their allowances just wouldn't stretch very far.

Beaver's father gave him a dollar a week, but this didn't mean he had a dollar to spend, because he had to put twenty cents in a piggy bank, so he would acquire the habit of saving. When there was a dollar in the piggy bank, it went into an account at a regular bank that was supposed to be the start of his college money.

Also, he gave a dime each week at Sunday school. So he really had only seventy cents a week to spend, instead of a dollar, and what with movies and a comic book every now and then, and occasional candy bars and malts, and bubble gum and donations to the Red Cross and poor kids in foreign countries, because Dad and Mom said everybody should do all they could for the unfortunate, Beaver just never had very much cash on hand. He knew that he probably couldn't save anything more from his allowance.

As for Wally, he had to put forty cents a week into a piggy bank and had all kinds of expenses. Beaver just didn't think Wally could save anything out of his allowance which was two dollars and a half a week because he was in high school.

Trailing along behind and thinking about all this, Beaver saw Wally and his two pals stop to

take a look at the car which was still in back of
Grimsby's garage. Then they went inside. But
only a couple of minutes later they came out
again, somewhat faster than they had gone in,
with Mr. Grimsby following them.

Mr. Grimsby was fat, like his son, and bald,
and red-faced. He was waving both arms and
yelling. "You kids get away from here and stay
away!" he shouted. "If you do any more meddling
with that car, I'll go to your folks!"

Sylvester was there, looking scared and trying
to say something. His father gave him a shove,
back toward the garage, and both of them went
inside again.

Wally and Eddie and Lumpy moved across
the street and stood on a corner for a minute.
They seemed to be arguing. Then Eddie and
Lumpy left together, and Wally headed off toward
town, head down and hands in pockets, scuffing
at the sidewalk.

Beaver was tempted to follow him and find out
what had happened, but he had a feeling that

Wally wouldn't want to talk about it just then. So, since there didn't seem to be anything else to do, Beaver went home again.

Mom told him dinner would be a little late. Dad did not return from his office, looking tired, until past six. Soon after that they were ready to eat, but Wally wasn't on hand.

"Where is that boy?" his father demanded.

"I don't know, dear," Mom said.

"I think he went downtown," Beaver volunteered.

"Well, he had better be in his chair here within the next couple of minutes," Dad said.

One thing Dad insisted on was that Wally and Beaver be prompt for all meals. But Wally didn't show up, and they had to start without him.

Then the phone rang, and Mom hurried to answer. She reported, coming back to the table, "Ward, it was Wally. He said not to worry, he is on his way home, and he apologized for not calling sooner, saying he hadn't realized how late it was. Also, he said that he has already eaten his dinner, and will have a big surprise for us when he gets here."

"Surprise?" Dad said, frowning.

"What in the world do you suppose he means?" Mom continued. "And how could he have had his dinner?"

"I haven't any idea, and I'm just as curious as you are, but we'll wait for Wally to tell us," Dad said. "Now, let's finish our own dinner."

Afterwards, Dad went into the den to work on some papers he had brought home while Beaver helped his mother with the dishes. Beaver could hardly wait to find out what Wally had been doing.

It was well past seven when the front door opened and Wally appeared. He went right into the den without having to be summoned, and Beaver edged in after him.

"Dad, the greatest thing ever happened to me this afternoon!" Wally exclaimed.

"Something has been happening here, too," Dad said. "Your mother and I have been disturbed and upset by your absence. Wally, you

know that on school nights you are supposed to
be home early—"

"Yes, sir, and I'm sorry for coming in late like
this," Wally said. "It just happened that way. And
I rushed home as fast as I could to tell you all
about it—"

"Tell us what?" Dad demanded. "Where have
you been and what have you been doing?"

"I've been working," Wally said. "I've got a
job!"

There was dead silence for a moment. Neither
Dad nor Mom seemed to have anything to say.

Wally started talking again. He had been walking along downtown and had seen a sign in a window, saying HELP WANTED. He had gone right in
and had applied for the job, and they had let him
try out for it. He had done all right, too, Wally
reported.

"It's washing dishes at the Busy Bee diner,"
Wally said. "I can work there after school for
two or three hours every day and as much as I
want to on weekends, and they'll pay me a dollar

an hour, plus whatever I want to eat. All I got tonight was my supper, because I was just trying out. I had some hamburgers and French fries and a couple of malteds."

"Oh, dear," Mom said faintly. "I don't think such food would be very good for you every night."

"The Busy Bee. That is the all-night diner on the boulevard, nearly two miles from here," Dad remarked.

"I took the bus home tonight but I'll walk after this to save money," Wally said. Then he hurried on. "I'll keep my school work up, Dad! I suppose that I'll have to quit the track team, but most of the meets are over anyway. Isn't it great, though!"

"I'm afraid I must disagree, Wally," Dad said. "I am also afraid you won't be going back to the Busy Bee."

"But, Dad!"

"You must call them and say you can't accept the job," his father told him.

Wally wore a sudden stunned look. "Why?" he cried.

Dad replied, "Son, the pay is too low for the work involved, no matter how many hamburgers and French fries and malteds they might let you consume. Besides, although I know you are very sincere in believing you could keep your school work up to the high standard necessary for you to go to college, and would try hard, I'm afraid there is too much risk you would find yourself slipping behind."

Beaver thought he had never seen his father so earnest about anything. And Dad continued, "I want you to know that I am pleased you went out and landed a job on your own. It shows you have a quality of initiative and ambition that will help you a lot, later on."

But Wally was thinking more about right now rather than what might happen later on. "I just want to make enough money so I can buy a car!" he said. "When I have it, I'll quit, Dad!"

"I know you mean that, also," Dad responded.

"When you did get the car, though, you would need money to fix it up and to drive it, with the temptation to keep on working. However, I am mostly concerned about the danger to your school grades. Don't you agree that nothing must prevent you from keeping a high average?"

Wally chewed his lip. After a moment he replied, low-voiced, "Yes, Dad."

"Then call the Busy Bee, son, and tell them you won't be back. You owe them that much."

Wally made the phone call. After it was completed he left the den, going upstairs.

There was silence in the den for a minute. Then Dad sighed ruefully. He said, "June, I suppose Wally isn't very happy with me right now. I don't feel very happy with myself. And don't remind me that you said he would find some way to try to earn money for that car!"

Mom said, "I won't. I was just remembering the time when you wanted to quit school and go to work in a service station, because you wanted money for something or other."

Dad said, "I hope you are also recalling that my father lowered the boom on me, to make sure I didn't do that, a lot harder than I just lowered it on Wally."

"Yes, dear," Mom said. "And Wally is a pretty sensible boy. I'm certain he will realize before long that you are completely right."

"I hope so," Dad said.

He laughed suddenly, and continued, "Washing dishes! Why, we almost have to use brute force to make him do them at home! I have a feeling Wally would soon have been very sick of such a job. But he seems to want a car so much I didn't dare to take a chance and let him go ahead, in the hope that would happen."

Mom noticed her younger son by the hall door. She said, "Upstairs, Beaver. This has been a rather trying day. All of us are going to turn in a little early."

So Beaver climbed the stairs to discover Wally lying on his bed, hands clasped under his head, staring at the ceiling.

"Sometimes I don't feel like I'll ever get anywhere, around here," Wally said moodily. "It's almost enough to make me go off and join the Marines!"

"Gosh, Wally, don't do that!" Beaver pleaded. "I would be too lonesome. And Mom would probably cry."

He had seen Mom cry a couple of times. It had made him feel all squeezed up and scared inside.

"I guess she would," Wally agreed. "And I didn't really mean it. But doggone everything, anyway!"

Beaver started to prepare for bed. He hadn't been able to do much homework this evening, but he felt too tired to get at it now. Mom was right. This had been quite a day.

"Wally—" he ventured, after a bit.

"Yeah?" his brother muttered.

"I kind of think maybe Dad was right, the things he said downstairs," Beaver told him.

"Sure, he was right," Wally agreed. "I've been thinking about it some, just now. That Busy Bee restaurant is a pretty crummy place, and its food isn't very good. It's awfully hot in the kitchen. Washing dishes there is real hard work, with people yelling at you all the time to hurry up. I thought maybe I could stand those things, because of the money I could make, and still keep up my school work, but after what Dad said I can see I was all wrong."

It seemed to Beaver a good time to ask what had happened at Grimsby's garage that afternoon.

"Why, I don't know, for sure," Wally told him. "Mr. Grimsby just started yelling before we could say anything, as though he thought we had been sneaking the car away from there to try it out. I tried to tell him we wouldn't do such a thing, but he wouldn't listen and chased us off, saying we had better not come back."

Wally got off his bed and went to study himself in a mirror, but without much interest. "I suppose I haven't got any chance at all of ever getting that heap now," he said.

He went to a window and looked out. "You

know something?" Wally went on. "Growing up is sure rough!"

Beaver considered this. Then a sudden startling thought occurred to him as he recalled all that Mom and Dad had been through today. He said, "Being grown up is pretty rough, too, sometimes!"

"I guess it is," Wally agreed.

"I don't s'pose there's anything we can do about it, though," Beaver said practically. "We've just got to go ahead and grow up whether we want to or not. G'night, Wally."

On the following afternoon when Beaver returned home from school he found Kit Markley waiting for him.

Beaver eyed the boy coldly. "You got me in a lot of trouble yesterday!" he said.

"I'm sorry," Kit Markley said.

Beaver sniffed. "I'll bet your folks told you to say that!"

"Well, they did," Kit admitted. "But I'm really sorry. It won't happen again."

"It had better not!" Beaver said.

Then he noticed that Kit seemed to be excited and on edge about something, and continued, "What's eating you, anyway?"

Words burst out of Kit. He had discovered that the cellar at his folks' house was full of bottles—hundreds of them, he claimed, maybe even thousands. Kit had asked his father if he and Beaver could have them, and Mr. Markley had said they might as well go right ahead.

"We'll make a lot of money!" Kit exclaimed. "You can get that bicycle real soon!"

Beaver refused to get very excited about it until he had a look for himself. He went with Kit to the Markley house. There he discovered that what Kit had told him was absolutely true.

Beaver had never seen so many bottles in one place in his life. He could tell at a glance that most of them were worth money.

All he had to do was haul them out of there, with Kit's help, and in no time at all he ought to have enough money to buy the English bike.

8
Getting Rich

The cellar under the Markley house was big and deep and sort of dark, with a steep, narrow flight of steps that led down to it from outside. Beaver couldn't believe his eyes for a minute when he saw the bottles. There were more bottles than Beaver had seen anywhere in his whole life.

They were everywhere, in boxes and cardboard cartons and stacked on shelves and just piled on the floor.

"Gosh!" Beaver said. "What are so many bottles doing here, anyway?"

Mr. Markley, who had accompanied them down to the cellar and who had turned on a light, said, "I don't really know, except that my folks never seemed to throw anything away, and I suppose it never occurred to anybody to collect the deposits that were due on them."

"You don't mind if we do the collecting?" Beaver asked. He wanted to be sure about this.

"I'll be delighted to get rid of them," Kit's father replied. He looked about the cellar, then. "As a matter of fact, there is a lot of other junk here. After you finish hauling the bottles away, I'll be glad to pay if you wish to clean the whole cellar out for me—and the attic, also."

It all semed too good to be true. Beaver felt like pinching himself. It looked now as though he could buy the bicycle in no time and even make some more money besides.

He might even be able to make enough to help Wally buy a car!

"I guess we had better get busy right away," Beaver decided.

"Go right to it," Mr. Markley said, and started up the flight of steep stairs. "Mind these steps, boys, going up and down. If you should slip, it might result in a hard fall."

Kit seemed very eager to start work. "What do we do first?" he asked.

"Well, this is liable to be sort of dirty work," Beaver said. "So first of all you had better go put on some old clothes."

He didn't want Mrs. Markley to become angry with him again if Kit got a little mussed up.

Kit looked surprised. "These are my old clothes!" he said.

Beaver had to laugh. What Kit was wearing looked almost as good as his own best suit. "Well, okay," he said. "I'll start sorting the bottles, and there's a big box yonder that we'll put them in. As soon as we get that box filled, we'll lug it upstairs."

Beaver had brought his wagon along. In no time at all they had the wagon jammed full. Then they hauled it to the supermarket and collected more than a dollar for the first load.

It hadn't taken very long, either. Beaver figured they could probably haul at least three or four loads this one afternoon alone, with plenty of bottles left in the cellar.

The Markley house was on the east side of the hollow, with a private driveway that led up to the street which crossed the bridge over the creek. It was only three blocks from the bridge to the supermarket.

Coming back, Beaver said, "That sure is a big old house you live in."

"Mama doesn't like it very much," Kit said. "I'm not sure yet whether we'll keep on living there. But I hope we will!"

Beaver had a feeling that what Kit was actually trying to say was that he didn't want to move away, now that he had found a friend.

Maybe everything was going to work out all right, Beaver thought. Kit was behaving differently today. He wasn't getting into trouble, and he was certainly working hard enough. Also, he was trying hard to learn things. He knew almost as much already as Beaver did about which bottles were worth money and which ones weren't.

They didn't go by the fire station, on their trips back and forth, but Kit spoke about the false alarm.

"I was too scared yesterday to go and say I was the one who turned it in," he told Beaver. "And I guess my father fixed things up so there won't be any trouble, but I kind of feel now that I ought to tell the firemen I did it."

Beaver remembered he had been scared, too. Kit, he thought, must have been twice as scared.

"I'll do that if you say so," Kit went on.

Beaver didn't quite know what to tell him.

He had an idea that his own father knew just about what had happened yesterday, and so did Mr. Markley. But Captain Gus had a feeling Beaver had somehow been involved in turning in the false alarm, because he had refused to say anything when questioned.

Beaver certainly did not want Captain Gus to go on feeling that way, but he also did not want anyone to think he had nudged Kit into confessing with the thought that he could get his own punishment lifted and could then go to the fire station again.

Maybe, Beaver thought, he should talk the whole thing over with Dad, who would know the right thing to do.

"You had better let me think about it for a while," he told Kit. "I'll let you know later."

"All right," Kit agreed.

On their third trip to the supermarket, the clerk at the check-stand laughed and said, "You kids must have found a bottle mine! But keep bringing them in, and I'll keep on paying!"

It was during the course of the third trip that Beaver saw Wally. His brother was standing across the street from Grimsby's place looking toward the garage and the car which still stood behind it. Wally hadn't given up, Beaver thought. He was still trying to figure some way to come into possession of that car.

Crossing the bridge a little later, he also had a glimpse of Aggie Moss. She was down in the hollow, dragging the box with the rope tied to it. The dirty little boy was with her.

"There's that mean old girl again," Kit remarked. "It looks like she's been hunting bottles again, too, the same as the last time we saw her."

"I s'pose so," Beaver agreed. Aggie seemed to be heading toward the shanties at the north end of the hollow.

Maybe, he thought, Aggie lived there, though this did not seem to be of any particular importance. All Beaver wanted, where Aggie Moss was concerned, was to stay as far away from her as he could.

The time was still fairly early, so he and Kit loaded up the wagon and made a fourth trip to the supermarket. By now, Beaver's pocket was bulging with the money they had collected. They trudged back and loaded the wagon still one more time.

Mrs. Markley came out of the house, however, before they could start a fifth trip, and said, "Boys, cook tells me dinner is almost ready. And —er—Beaver, you're to be our guest. I called your mother. She said it will be all right for you to dine with us."

"Thank you, ma'am," he said politely.

He decided it would be all right to leave the wagon with its load of bottles outside of the house. Maybe there would be time later to take it to the supermarket. This was a Friday evening and he didn't have to hurry home since there was no need to study tonight.

Kit led the way up to his room. Beaver looked about with astonishment. "You've got just about everything!" he exclaimed.

"I guess so," Kit replied.

Kit had his own TV set and a short-wave radio, too. He had books and all sorts of games, and a telescope, and a camera which developed its own pictures. He also had stuff to draw and paint with, and a big drawing table. It all had the look of having cost a lot.

At the same time, though, everything also had a sort of unused look. Beaver had a feeling that Kit owned so much he hadn't gotten around to doing very much with any of it.

Both of them were dirty from handling so many dusty bottles. They washed up. Then Beaver counted out the money they had made, more than five dollars, and gave Kit half of it.

Kit held his share. "Is this very much, for the work we did?" he asked.

"It sure is!" Beaver replied. It was more money than he had ever been able to make in such a short time for doing anything.

They went downstairs. The Markleys were waiting in a big dining room that was rather dark even though all of the lights were on. Beaver was shown his place at one side of a long dining table. Kit was on the other side. Mr. Markley sat at one end of the table and Mrs. Markley at the other.

A maid who wore a white apron and a frilly cap waited on them. The food was all right, though not nearly as good as Mom's cooking. Beaver was very careful about his manners. Mom had taught him how to act when he was in somebody else's home, and he wasn't going to do anything that might make her feel ashamed of him.

Dinner here was rather strange, not at all like dinner at home. Beaver was mannerly enough there, too, of course, and so was Wally. Mom and Dad saw to that. But there was a lot of talk and laughter at their dining table, and always a warm, comfortable feeling.

Nobody said much for quite a while. Beaver felt a little stiff and strained. He noticed that Mrs. Markley wasn't eating anything, but was just poking at her food.

But, after a while Mr. Markley asked how they had made out with the bottles, and Kit started talking. He told all about the afternoon's work, including the money they had made, and did a little bragging, making it seem again that he had done more than had actually been the case.

Beaver didn't mind, because Kit's parents seemed so pleased. Mr. Markley beamed at his son. He said, "I'm very glad you're learning what it takes to earn a dollar, Kit. And I am hopeful you will enjoy this money you have made much more than any that is just handed to you."

Mrs. Markley smiled, also. "I'm so proud of you, dear," she said. "I think you deserve an additional reward for all of your hard work, and I'll try to think of a present that is appropriate."

Beaver supposed this meant that Kit would get something more to add to his many possessions upstairs, and wondered whether it would have any meaning as far as the other boy was concerned. Kit had so much already.

Beaver waited in a long front hall after dinner while Kit went upstairs to get his jacket. The Markleys were still at the table in the dining room with the door open. All at once he heard Mr. Markley say, "Please keep trying, Enid!"

Then Mrs. Markley spoke, her voice raised. "I am trying, Bob, because you say it is important for Kit's sake that we stay in one place for a while, that he make some friends and grow up normally. But I never did like this gloomy old house and I don't like it now. I—I just don't know if I can keep on living here!"

"It was once my home. I would like it to be Kit's home, too," Mr. Markley said. "But we'll see."

Kit came downstairs. They went outside and found that the wagon with its load of bottles was gone.

Kit said, "Maybe Clarkson—he's our chauffeur —moved your wagon away."

Beaver studied the tracks left by the wagon's wheels. They slanted off from the house in the direction of the shanties at the north end of the hollow.

"No, sir!" he said. "Somebody came along, saw those bottles and just walked off with them. I'll bet I know who it was, too—Aggie Moss! Well, she isn't going to get away with it!"

The girl who had caused him so much trouble had gone too far this time. Beaver started running, following the tracks made by his wagon.

"Come on!" he called over his shoulder to Kit. "We'll find her and tell Aggie to give everything back! If she doesn't—well, she'd just better!"

9
Aggie's Story

The shanties were about a half a mile from the Markley house. Beaver saw, approaching them, that they were little shacks made out of scraps of wood, pieces of tin, and strips of canvas. They were in under some trees and close to the bank of the creek.

Several outdoor fires were burning with people cooking their suppers. Dad had said times were hard for such folks, who had nowhere else to live, with talk in the town that something ought to be done for them, but nothing had been done so far.

Beaver began to wonder about Aggie Moss living in one of the shacks. But he could think about that later. Right now, he wanted his wagon and the bottles, and it didn't take long to find them. They were beside a shack that was right on the bank of the creek.

Kit, who had caught up with him, said, "Maybe we'd just better take the wagon and leave. I don't want to hang around here. I don't think I like this place!"

Beaver hesitated. He didn't care for being among the shanties, either. Seeing people who had to live in such a fashion gave him a crawly feeling.

Before he could make up his mind Aggie Moss suddenly appeared, hurrying among the trees toward the shack where he had spied his wagon.

She was instantly very angry. "What are you snooping around here for, Beaver Cleaver?" Aggie cried. "You beat it! And don't you dare come back!"

Beaver flared up, in turn. "That's a fine way to talk, after taking something that doesn't belong to you! We could have told the police, and you'd be in plenty of trouble!"

Aggie stared at him. "What are you talking about?"

Beaver said scornfully, "As if you didn't know!" He pointed to his wagon. "That's what I'm talking about! You saw those bottles, and you walked off with them!"

Aggie stared now at the wagon. Then she suddenly turned and plunged at the shack's door, jerking it open. She rushed inside, crying out, "Billy! I want to talk to you!"

Beaver followed her. He stood at the open doorway looking in.

It was a small place, only one room, cluttered with stuff. There was a table and some chairs, and a bed at one side with a little girl sitting in the middle of it. She had on what looked like a night-gown and was sucking on her thumb. Staring at Beaver with very big eyes, the child appeared not much more than two or three years old.

Aggie was with the little boy whom he had seen twice before, helping her to pull the box in which she put the bottles that she found. Aggie had hold of his shoulder and was shaking him.

"Billy, I've told you we don't ever touch anything that might belong to somebody!" Aggie
cried. "We only pick up stuff that people throw
away!"

The little boy—he was about six, Beaver
thought, and very thin and scrawny—began to
cry.

"We haven't got anything to eat, and couldn't
find anything to sell today," the boy whimpered.
"I had to take those bottles, Aggie. I'm hungry!"

"We'll starve before we steal anything!" Aggie
said fiercely. "And I saw a trash pile today where
there ought to be some stuff I can sell. I'll go and
check on it tonight, when there won't be anybody around to notice and maybe report us to the
charity people."

She let the boy go. "I found a potato, back of
a store," Aggie continued. "I'll boil it, and you
and Jennie can each have half for your supper.
Then, tomorrow, there'll be more to eat. We're
going to make out, Billy, and stay together some

way. We'll do it without taking anything that isn't ours!"

Kit was standing just behind Beaver, looking on also, but he didn't have anything to say. Neither did Beaver, for that matter.

Aggie turned to them. "I'm sorry," she said. "I apologize for Billy. He wouldn't have taken your bottles if I had been around. He's just a little boy, and he doesn't understand about some things. I—I hope you won't be hard on him."

This was an Aggie Moss who was quite a bit different from the one Beaver had known at school.

"I guess we don't want to be hard on anybody, Aggie," he said.

"And don't tell about seeing us here," Aggie begged. "Please don't!"

She was scared, Beaver realized. It was terribly important to Aggie that nobody should know how she and these other two were living.

"Okay," Beaver agreed. "We won't."

"Thanks," Aggie said. "And I'm sorry I was

always so mean to you, Beaver. It was because you have so much and I don't have anything."

"So much?" Beaver said, greatly surprised.

"You have nice folks, and you live in a big house, and you never have to worry about anything," Aggie said. "It was wrong of me to grudge you all you've got, though, to be mean and to snitch on you so much. It won't happen again. I won't ever snitch on anybody from now on. I promise!"

Beaver couldn't seem to think of anything more to say. Kit indicated that he wanted to leave, but Beaver did not pay attention to him.

After a moment, Aggie spoke again. "Just take your wagon and get out of here!"

Instead, Beaver took a step into the shanty. He looked around once more. "I guess these little kids are your brother and sister," he said.

Aggie nodded jerkily.

"Listen, is a potato really all they're going to have for supper?" Beaver said. "It doesn't seem like very much. And what are you going to eat,

Aggie? You're hungry, too."

"Never mind about me!" Aggie Moss cried. "Go away and forget that you were ever here!"

Beaver did not move, though. He couldn't, for some reason.

Suddenly the little girl in the bed took her thumb out of her mouth and started to wail, a thin, pleading sort of sound.

Aggie looked toward the child. Her features seemed to crumple. She reached for a chair and sat down at the table. Aggie put her hands to her face and began to cry.

"I can take it," she wept. "But poor Billy and Jennie—it's so awful hard on them."

Beaver felt as he had when he had seen Mom cry, all twisted and churned up inside. He went to Aggie and put a hand on her arm. "Please don't do that," he begged. "Please don't, Aggie!"

Kit Markley was standing in the doorway looking uneasy. "Listen, it's starting to get dark," he said.

Beaver ignored him. Then, after a moment,

but realized immediately that he could think for a week and the answer would still be the same. Beaver dug into his pocket for his share of the money made from selling bottles in the afternoon. He placed the money on the table in front of Aggie.

"You take this and spend it for whatever you need," Beaver said. "And I'll bring you some more tomorrow."

He and Kit had all day tomorrow in which to work. Maybe they could clean out all of the rest of the bottles in the cellar, and he should then have a lot of cash to use in helping Aggie Moss.

Kit had made a startled sound behind him as he put his share of today's hard work in front of Aggie.

She stared at the money, wide-eyed. "It's awful nice of you, Beaver," Aggie said. "I—I can't take this, though."

"Sure, you can," Beaver told her. "I want you to have it."

"Well," Aggie said, drawing a deep, unsteady

breath, "I'll take it for Billy and Jennie then, not for myself. I'll go out and get some soup and bread, some medicine, too. And I'll do the best I can to pay you back, just as soon as possible!"

Beaver doubted that she could do this. He wasn't expecting to get any of it back.

He glanced around to Kit and said, "Uh—if you want to do something, too—"

"All I want is to get out of here!" Kit said.

Beaver and Kit returned to the Markley place from the shanties a few minutes later. Beaver was pulling the wagon, planning to leave it beside the cellar door. He felt too tired to haul its load of bottles to the supermarket.

Kit did not speak until they reached the house. Then he remarked, "You're never going to get that bicycle if you give all of your money away."

"Maybe not," Beaver said. "But it looks like somebody has got to help Aggie and those little kids."

Kit made no response to this. Beaver felt a little

stiff toward him, and a little angry as well.

Of course, it was none of his business what Kit did with his share of the money they had made thus far. Beaver couldn't help but feel, though, that it wouldn't have hurt the other boy to offer Aggie a little something, also. Kit, who had so much of everything, would hardly have missed it.

He hadn't even said he was sorry for Aggie and hoped everything would be all right.

It was nearly dark now, very cloudy, though it wasn't raining.

Kit spoke again. "I suppose you'll be here the first thing in the morning?"

"I s'pose so," Beaver agreed. "G'night."

He trudged away, up the driveway to the street at the east side of the hollow and on toward the bridge.

Beaver still felt angry toward the other boy. He had a sudden feeling that he and Kit Markley just didn't look at things the same way and never would, that they couldn't ever be friends.

Then he remembered his talks with Dad, and

felt a little ashamed of himself, with the realization that he would be letting his father down if he gave up on Kit so soon.

Maybe he would be letting Kit down, too. Beaver didn't know. It all seemed very confusing.

By tomorrow, though, everything might be a lot better, all the way around. Beaver hoped so, beginning to hurry now because he was anxious to get home.

10
Too Much
to Bear

Mom and Dad were out, calling on friends. Wally, wearing his best suit and one of Dad's neckties, was carefully combing his hair. He had collected his allowance and was going somewhere. Since this was a Friday night, Wally would be allowed to stay out a little later than usual.

Beaver asked, "Are you going to stand around in front of that girl's house for a while?"

"No!" Wally replied. "And if you tell anybody that I ever did, I'll really make things hot for you!"

He left. Beaver wished he hadn't riled Wally up. He had wanted to talk to his brother about what he had done for Aggie Moss and Kit's failure to do anything. Beaver felt pretty sure Wally would feel the same way he did, but wanted to hear him say so. And maybe Wally could give him some advice about what he should do tomorrow.

He had to discuss with Dad about whether Kit should tell Captain Gus that turning in the false alarm was solely Kit's responsibility. But Beaver felt so tired after all of today's hard work that he couldn't keep his eyes open, and it wasn't yet nine o'clock when he went up to bed.

Mom was there, after a while, to tuck him in. Beaver was drowsily aware of this, and of Wally coming quietly into the room and also going to bed, later.

Much later, he was aware of thunder, and of rain beating against the house.

Then it was morning, still raining, and Dad was coming in, already dressed, saying, "Wally, get up, put your clothes on and come downstairs. Immediately!"

Dad's features were tight and strained. There was a tone in his voice that Beaver had never heard before. He sat up, as Wally was hurriedly getting dressed, and said, "What do you s'pose has happened?"

"I don't know," Wally replied, looking puzzled.

As Wally left the room, Beaver put on his bathrobe and went out to the stairs. He didn't have to go any farther. He could see and hear everything from there.

Mr. Grimsby was standing in the lower hall, facing Wally and Dad, with Mom nearby.

Wally was saying, "Honest, Mr. Grimsby, I didn't smash up your car!"

"Somebody did," Mr. Grimsby said. "Somebody took it out last night after I closed up, probably a little after eight o'clock—it was seen about then, heading south on Main Street—and skidded off the river road, right into a concrete pillar where they're building the new bridge. The car wasn't insured and is a total loss. Whoever drove it is going to pay!"

"But it wasn't me!" Wally protested. "I wasn't anywhere near your garage last night!"

"Well," Mr. Grimsby said, "you and two other kids have been fooling around that car all of this past week. I have already checked on the other two, the Haskell and Rutherford boys. They were both at home with their folks all of last evening. Where were you?"

"I—I was downtown," Wally replied. "I came home about ten o'clock."

Dad put in a question. "Whereabouts downtown, son?"

"I went to the library," Wally told him. "But I didn't go in the library. I was sort of outside of it."

"Outside?" Dad said. "With someone?"

"No, sir, I wasn't with anybody," Wally answered. "And I don't think anybody saw me, either. I—I just don't think I can prove I was there, Dad."

There was a moment of silence. Then Mr. Grimsby said, "Cleaver, I don't feel I can be blamed for what I am thinking. This boy of yours took my car out for a joyride last night and smashed it up."

"You have no proof of that," Dad said quietly, but with strength in his voice.

"I haven't heard any proof that it didn't happen," Mr. Grimsby said, "or that he didn't leave the car and come home, hoping nobody would ever know it was his doing, letting me find out from the Highway Patrol when they discovered the wreck at three o'clock this morning."

"I didn't do any of those things!" Wally said, sounding desperate.

"Young man, I'd say it was up to you to produce somebody to back up that statement, and you evidently can't," Mr. Grimsby said. "Now, I mean to collect for my wrecked car—four hundred dollars!"

"Four hundred? But Sylvester told us you would sell it for a hundred!" Wally cried.

"Sylvester? He didn't know what he was talking about!" Mr. Grimsby snorted. "I took the car on a trade-in for four hundred dollars. I have the papers to show what it cost me, and that is what I am going to collect!"

Dad said, "I will always pay this family's just debts. But Wally has said he had nothing to do with wrecking your car. I accept his statement as true."

"You had better think twice about that," Mr. Grimsby said warningly. "I have a son of my own and know the fix you're in, so I don't want to be hard on you. But unless I am paid, and pretty quick, I'll have to go to the law. I don't think you want me to do that, because of what a judge and jury might say about the story your son tells concerning where he was last night!"

Mr. Grimsby left quickly, then, closing the front door behind him.

Dad said, a minute or so later, "Wally, exactly what did you do last night? You say that you went to the library, but did not go inside?"

"Yes, sir," Wally replied. "I stopped at that little park next door to it. There wasn't anybody around, and I don't think they'd have seen me if there had been, because I was kind of standing under some trees."

Mom said, "Dear, were you waiting for a friend?"

"That's the way it was, Mom," Wally said, sounding grateful because she had spoken. "Only this friend didn't know I was there—and didn't show up."

"You stood under some trees waiting for somebody who might come along?" Dad said. "How long did you do that?"

"Well, I guess I must have done it for at least a couple of hours," Wally replied.

Neither Dad nor Mom seemed to have anything to say, then. And Wally went on, "I can't help the way it sounds! I'm telling you the truth!"

Mom said, "We'll all have some breakfast, and then we'll feel better."

"I couldn't eat anything," Wally said. "May I go back to my room? Please!"

Dad nodded permission, and Wally came upstairs, past Beaver.

After a moment, Mom said, "Ward, I know his story seems strange, but Wally has never lied to us, and he isn't doing that now."

"June, I believe him," Dad said. "A boy who was really guilty would not have behaved the way Wally did—and would have a much more plausible story ready to tell us, too!"

Mom said, "Can Mr. Grimsby make trouble for us, as he threatened?"

"I'm afraid so," Dad replied. "He can sue us, claiming that Wally wrecked his car. If he were to win—and there is no telling what a jury might decide—he could collect his four hundred dollars, plus all court costs."

"Oh!" Mom said. "We would have to pay—?"

"Yes. Fortunately, the money is available, though it would take all that I have set aside for our vacation trip this summer," Dad told her.

Beaver felt his heart sink at the thought of this happening.

Then Dad went on strongly, "But I don't mean for it to go that far! Somebody must have noticed Wally last night, when Grimsby says he was driving the car. Right after breakfast I'll go downtown and start questioning everybody who might possibly have seen him!"

Beaver went to get dressed.

Wally was lying on his bed, staring at the ceiling again. Beaver said, "Everything is going to be all right, Wally!" He told about Dad's plan to find somebody who had seen him.

"It won't do any good," Wally muttered. "Like I said, I was standing under some trees. It was real dark there, and nobody came along. I sure wish Dad could find somebody who saw me, but I've got a feeling that it just isn't going to happen."

"Wally, why did you stand around under those trees for so long?" Beaver asked.

"Never mind," his brother said, then turned on his side away from Beaver. "And the way I feel, I'd like to be by myself. Go away and leave me alone, Beave, please."

It seemed to Beaver that this was the longest day he had ever experienced.

The rain kept coming down, harder and harder, so that he couldn't go to the Markley house and finish taking the bottles out of the cellar to collect on them, even if he had been in a mood to do that.

Beaver decided that he ought to call and explain that he wouldn't be along, so he dialed the Markley number, but an operator told him the phone there was out of order.

Wally stayed in his room. Mom took some food up to him, then came back and said he didn't want to talk to her, either.

Dad was away until past two in the afternoon. He was wet and tired when he returned, and Beaver needed only one look at his face to realize Wally had been right, that Dad hadn't been able to find anybody who could back up his story of where he had been when Mr. Grimsby's car had been driven away from the garage.

"It's pretty difficult just to get about," Dad reported. "Most of the streets downtown are flooded, and I hear people on the south side are becoming concerned, afraid the creek that runs through the hollow will overflow and flood their places, too."

He had his lunch, then went up to speak to Wally. He came down again shaking his head and left, saying he had to find a night watchman of a building across from the library park who might have seen Wally.

The afternoon passed slowly, and now Beaver began to worry about Aggie Moss. She and her little brother and sister could be in real danger if the creek overflowed. Their shanty was right on its bank.

It began to seem, however, that his worry was needless, for along toward six o'clock the rain started to let up. Then it stopped altogether.

Mom asked if he would go to the supermarket and get some things she needed. Beaver was glad to have a chance to be out of the house for a while. He put on his jacket and cap, also his rubbers, though he disliked wearing them.

Mom insisted on the rubbers. "We have enough trouble already without you picking up a cold," she said. "And no wading in the gutters!"

All of the gutters were certainly full, Beaver

noticed as he hurried toward the supermarket. Thick black clouds still hung low, and it was going to be dark before very long.

He encountered Eddie Haskell and Lumpy Rutherford. They told how Mr. Grimsby had hammered at their front doors, early in the morning. Then they wanted to know what had happened when he had arrived at the Cleaver house.

Beaver told them, but left out the part about Wally standing under the trees in the library park, since he had an idea his brother wouldn't want that talked about.

He said instead that Wally had been downtown yesterday evening and that Dad was now trying to find somebody who might have seen him at the time when Mr. Grimsby's car was being driven away from the garage.

Lumpy said, "Well, I caught it good from my dad just because I had fooled around that old heap some."

"So did I," Eddie Haskell said. "My father hasn't yelled at me so loud in quite a while. I

guess it is a mighty good thing for us that we were
both at home all evening last night!"

Beaver said, "I'll bet both of your dads would
be standing up for you, though, if you were in
trouble, the same way our dad is standing up for
Wally."

They nodded in sober agreement. Then Lumpy
said, "Listen, Beaver, you tell Wally we're hoping
that everything works out okay for him."

"That's right," Eddie said. "Also, tell him to
let us know if there is anything at all we can do
to help out."

Beaver promised that he would and went on to
the supermarket. He picked up the things on the
list Mom had given him and started back.

All at once he discovered that, without even
thinking about it, absorbed as he was in worrying
about Wally, he was taking a return route that
was leading him right past Mr. Hallam's shop.
Then he saw the show window was empty. The
bike was gone.

Beaver rushed inside, hoping it had only been

taken out of the window for Mr. Hallam to do something to it.

But the owner of the shop, who was repairing an electric toaster at his workbench, said, "I told you I would have to sell the bicycle, Beaver, if somebody came along with the money to buy it, and that is just what happened—only a little while ago, too."

"Can you tell me wh-who it was?" Beaver asked.

"A very nice lady," Mr. Hallam replied. "She said that she was getting it for her son. I wrote out a receipt. Where is my copy, now?" He looked about his cluttered shop. "Oh, yes, there it is."

Mr. Hallam picked up a piece of paper. He said, "It was purchased by a Mrs. Robert Markley."

Beaver felt suddenly sick inside.

To learn that the bicycle was gone and beyond his reach was bad enough. But to discover, also, that it now belonged to Kit Markley was almost more than Beaver Cleaver could take.

11

Kit Disappears

It was starting to rain again, only a drizzle but with rumblings of thunder and flashes of lightning which indicated it was likely to come down harder before very long.

Beaver walked homeward scuffing at the sidewalk. He didn't care how hard it rained, didn't much care about anything except what he had learned at Mr. Hallam's shop.

Beaver still felt sick inside and very angry at Kit Markley.

He supposed that maybe Kit had decided he might as well have the bicycle for himself, after Beaver had seemingly given up his chance for it by handing the money he had earned to Aggie

Moss and saying he meant to give her more, also.

Kit must have asked his mother for it and she had gotten it for him the way Kit had said she got him just about anything he wanted. The bicycle would be added to his other possessions. None of them meant much to him and the bike probably wouldn't, either—not anywhere near what it meant to Beaver.

No matter how it had happened, though, Kit had done something which Beaver felt he could never forget or forgive. "Doggone him, anyway!" he said bitterly.

He remembered how he had hoped Kit could keep on living at the big house in the hollow. Now he wished the boy would go far away and never come back.

He turned in at the Cleaver driveway and let himself into the house through the kitchen door.

Everything seemed to be very quiet. Beaver placed the bag of groceries on the sink drainboard and went on to the front, where he found Wally standing by a window, looking out.

"Dad came by but went away again," Wally said. "Mom went with him. They're going to talk to a lawyer. I think the way it is going to wind up is that Dad will have to pay Mr. Grimsby the money."

Beaver felt ashamed of himself for having forgotten about Wally for a while as he thought about the bicycle and Kit Markley. Wally's troubles were certainly a lot more important than his.

"I—I sure hoped hard that Dad could find somebody who saw you last night, Wally!" he said.

"So did I, even though I felt all the time it wasn't much use doing any hoping," Wally muttered.

He started to pace back and forth moodily. "All I ever did was to try to figure out some way I could buy that heap," Wally said. "I never even thought of driving it without Mr. Grimsby knowing, like he says I did!"

"I know you didn't, Wally," Beaver said. "Mom

and Dad know it, too. They believe you."

"Well, Dad is still going to have to pay because it was wrecked, and that means there won't be any vacation trip this summer, all on account of me," Wally said.

"I don't think Mom and Dad will mind," Beaver told him. "I won't, either."

"Thanks for saying that, Beave," Wally said. "But Dad shouldn't have to pay anything! It's all so doggoned unfair!"

He went to look out of the window. Rain pitter-pattered against the pane.

"There's no use griping about it, though," Wally continued. "And what I've got to do is to make it up to all of you. I've been thinking hard ever since this morning, and decided there is only one thing I can do. So I called the Busy Bee restaurant a while ago. They said the dishwashing job there is still open, and I can have it. I'm going to work."

Beaver did not think Dad would be any more in favor of Wally taking the dishwashing job than he had been before, and said so.

"He's just got to let me do it, this time," Wally said determinedly. "It's a pretty crummy job, but I don't know where I can get another one. And I'm going to pay back every cent that Dad has to put out on account of me!"

Beaver felt very sorry for him, and tried to think of some way to cheer Wally up. He told about running into Eddie and Lumpy, and their message.

"They're pretty good guys," Wally said, "even if Lumpy is kind of slow-thinking and Eddie is always full of slick talk. I guess I won't be seeing them very much after I go to work."

Thinking about this obviously depressed him even more than ever. Beaver, still trying to cheer him up, said, "I'll play you a game of checkers if you want to."

Wally did not answer.

"I could fix us some peanut butter and jelly sandwiches," Beaver persisted.

"Thanks, Beave, but I don't guess so," Wally

said. "All I want to do is figure out what I'm going to say to Dad, that he has to let me take the dishwashing job so I can pay back the money that he'll have to hand over to Mr. Grimsby."

Beaver said, "I s'pose it would take an awfully long time for you to pay back four hundred dollars?"

"More than a year, I expect," Wally said.

Beaver realized he probably wouldn't see very much of Wally after he started to work. Also, if it took more than a year maybe Wally would have to quit school, with things happening so he could never go back. And for Wally, with his ambition and plans for college, this would be a terrible blow.

"It's all on account of that Mr. Grimsby and his old car!" Beaver cried angrily. "I don't think it was worth any four hundred dollars. I'll bet it wasn't even worth a hundred!"

"No, I guess it cost him what he said," Wally replied.

"Maybe we could find out who wrecked it!"

Beaver cried in sudden excitement, wondering why he hadn't thought of this before. "Let's go out and ask around, Wally! Somebody must have seen who was driving it!"

But Wally shook his head. "Dad already thought of that. He talked to the Highway Patrol, who had checked but couldn't find anybody that saw who was driving it. I think the key was in the ignition—like it was every time I fooled around the heap—and somebody just came along, saw the key, and decided to take a ride. The Highway Patrol says it is a wonder nobody got hurt, but they couldn't find any sign of that. The car hit the bridge pillar sideways and practically broke in two. Dad says he saw it, and it's a complete wreck."

"Well—" Beaver said uncertainly, not knowing anything more to suggest.

Wally sighed. "I guess we won't ever know who did take the heap out," he said.

The phone rang suddenly. Wally went to answer. Beaver supposed it was either Mom or

Dad, but Wally called, "It's Mr. Markley, Beave, and he wants to talk to you."

Beaver took the phone and heard the voice of Mr. Markley, sounding strained and anxious, asking, "Is Kit there with you, Beaver?"

"Why, no, sir," Beaver answered. "I haven't seen him all day."

"He disappeared from the house some time ago. With the rain and the creek overflowing its banks, his mother is almost frantic with worry," Mr. Markley said. "Do you have any idea where he might have gone?"

Beaver had to say no in reply to that question, also.

"I have searched along the creek toward the bridge, and under it," Mr. Markley said. "I'm calling from a phone near the bridge since our phone at the house is out of order. Beaver, if Kit should show up at your house, will you tell him to come home at once?"

"Yes, sir," Beaver replied, though in his opinion the Cleaver house was the last place where Kit was likely to show up, after what he had done about the bicycle.

"Thank you," Mr. Markley said. "I—I know I can depend on you."

He hung up. So did Beaver. Mr. Markley had sounded real scared, he thought.

"What was that all about?" Wally asked.

Beaver told him. Wally said, "Can Kit Markley swim?"

"I don't know," Beaver replied.

"Well, it might not make much difference whether he can or not," Wally went on. "That creek is pretty rough when there is a flood. If he fell in it, he might be swept down to the river and never get out."

Beaver shivered. The thought of falling in the creek when it was flooding gave him goose bumps. He had seen the creek that way once, transformed into a roaring monster of a stream. The river into which it flowed, a mile south of the bridge, was even worse after a heavy rain.

Beaver went to a window and looked out. It

wasn't quite dark yet, and the rain still wasn't coming down very hard. He said, "Listen, Wally, Mr. Markley has been pretty nice to me, and Mrs. Markley, too. I kind of have a feeling that I ought to go to their place. Maybe there is something I can do to help out."

"Gosh, I don't know about that, Beave," Wally said. "I don't think Mom and Dad would want you to go out, with it almost dark and no telling how hard it might rain. I especially don't think they would want you to go anywhere near the creek tonight."

"I don't guess they would," Beaver agreed. "But Dad says there are times when you've just got to do something because you know down deep that it's right, and that's how I feel now."

"If you put it that way, I guess you'd better go," Wally decided.

"When Mom and Dad get home you can tell them where I am," Beaver said. "I'm pretty sure they'll want to head for the Markleys and help out, too, if they can."

"No, I think I had better go with you," Wally said. "We'll leave them a note."

Wally put on his leather jacket and an old hat he had used the previous summer while fishing during the Cleavers' vacation trip. He wrote a note and pinned it to the door of the den, where Mom and Dad would be sure to see it as soon as they returned.

Then he and Beaver set out, hurrying along deserted, rain-swept streets. Beaver was very glad Wally was along—and it was like his brother to put aside his own troubles and help out, he thought, even though Wally hardly knew Kit Markley at all.

They came to the bridge and crossed it, then slid down the ravine bank on the other side. They could see the creek now, covering half of the hollow, making a great booming roar where it poured under the bridge.

"I can't remember ever seeing it any higher than it is right now," Wally muttered.

"I s'pose we had better head right for the

Markley house," Beaver said. "Then—"

But he fell silent, because somebody was coming toward them, carrying a lantern. It was Mr. Markley, Beaver discovered, holding up the lantern to look them over and obviously startled to see them. His face was white and strained. Beaver hurriedly explained why he and Wally had come to the hollow.

"It is very kind of you boys to offer to help. And I haven't found him," Kit's father said. "I've just taken a look into the old mine that I dug years ago. I hadn't gotten around to boarding that up once more and I thought Kit might possibly have fallen in again, and couldn't get out. But the hole there is empty."

Beaver shivered again. He was thinking of Kit Markley and of the rain-swollen creek. Maybe, Beaver told himself, nobody would ever see Kit again.

12
Flood!

Rain splashed against Beaver's face. It was now quite dark. He looked toward the Markley house, in the near distance, and saw a number of lights there in various rooms.

He also noticed a car outside of the house. Its headlights were on, pointing up the private driveway toward the street at the top of the hollow's east bank, and he asked Kit's father about it.

"A mud slide has covered the drive. I can't get the car out to the street," Mr. Markley replied. "I have the headlights on so that if Kit returns by way of the street he will see the mud slide and can go around it."

Wally asked then if he had looked through

the trees on the other side of the creek near the bridge.

"Yes," Kit's father replied. "I didn't find a thing."

"How about the north end of the hollow?" Wally continued. "Did you look there?"

"No," Mr. Markley replied.

Beaver glanced in that direction. He noticed several lights moving about among the shanties and thought he heard distant sounds of people shouting.

Mr. Markley went on, "I happened to notice yesterday for the first time that some squatters are apparently living at that end of the hollow, beyond the city limits. I can't imagine any reason why Kit should have gone there, however."

"Somebody ought to look for him at that end of the hollow, though, just to make sure," Wally said.

Beaver looked again toward the Markley house. There was something about it that perhaps should be checked, he thought, but he couldn't quite decide what it was.

"I suppose you are right," Mr. Markley replied to Wally. He sounded anxious and uncertain.

"If it's okay with you, Mr. Markley, we'll all go and see if Kit is at those shanties," Wally continued. "And if he isn't—well, I think you and I had better start looking along the creek south of the bridge while Beaver goes to bring help—a lot of help. He'll have to do that, because he said your phone is out of order."

Mr. Markley said, "South of the bridge—?" He sounded desperate now, as though he had been trying hard not to believe Kit might have fallen into the creek and had been swept under the bridge toward the river.

That was when Beaver realized what there was at the house that ought to be checked, a glow of illumination almost at ground level on this side. He said, "Mr. Markley, did you turn the light on in your cellar tonight?"

Kit's father stared at him. "In the cellar? No,

I haven't been down there since yesterday afternoon, when you and Kit started taking those bottles out."

"Well, I think the light is on," Beaver said, pointing toward it.

Mr. Markley turned to look toward the house. "By George, it is!" he exclaimed.

"Maybe Kit went down there to sort out the rest of those bottles," Beaver said. "Maybe he didn't know you were looking for him and is down in the cellar now!"

"I—I hope you're right," Mr. Markley said. "Come on; we'll find out for sure!"

He rushed away, his lantern swinging back and forth. Wally started to follow him, but Beaver plucked at his brother's sleeve. "I'm going to those shanties first, Wally," he said. "I wish you'd go with me."

"Why do that?" Wally objected. "If Kit is in the cellar, we won't have to do any more looking."

"I've got another reason," Beaver told him and hurriedly explained about Aggie Moss and her brother and sister, about what had happened yesterday and his renewed fear that they might be in trouble in their shanty that was right on the creek bank.

Wally offered no further objection. "Sure, you've got to check on them," he agreed. "It had better be done fast, too, because it sounds like that creek is getting higher all the time."

They started toward the shanties, staying well on the east side of the creek. The rain continued to fall steadily. A hard wind was beginning to blow, whipping raindrops stingingly at their faces. It was pretty dark and scary in the hollow, and Beaver was very glad that Wally was with him.

He told how he had wanted to talk to his brother last night, telling about giving Aggie Moss the money and checking with Wally as to whether it had been the right thing for him to do.

"Gee, Beave, I don't see how you could have just walked away leaving little kids who were hungry," Wally said. "I think anybody would have done exactly what you did."

"Kit Markley didn't do it," Beaver pointed out.

"He sounds like a strange kind of guy," Wally said. "And from the way you say he acted last night, it looks like I was all wrong in thinking he might be at those shanties."

"Gosh, Wally, maybe his Dad won't find him in their cellar, either," Beaver said.

"Well, I'm afraid there'll be only one answer then as to what happened to him," Wally replied.

Beaver felt the same fear, that Kit Markley had somehow fallen into the creek and hadn't been able to pull himself out again.

Then the two of them were in among the shanties, where people were rushing around, shouting to each other, with a few flashlights and lanterns shining in the darkness. The ones who lived here were being flooded out and were trying to salvage as many of their belongings as they could, carrying them to higher ground.

Beaver felt water rise above his ankles, then toward his knees, cold water that was running fast, shoving at him. Wally grabbed his hand, as they splashed toward the Moss shanty. "Hold on!" he yelled.

Beaver did not need to be warned. If the water got any deeper, if he was swept off his feet and away from Wally, he could be in great danger.

The door of the Moss shanty was standing open. A dim light was shining within. Aggie's little brother Billy came splashing out, carrying a chair, and hurried off into the darkness with it.

Beaver and Wally reached the door and looked in.

The bed was already gone. Aggie was struggling in an effort to push the table toward the door. Several cloth-wrapped bundles were piled up on it.

Somebody was helping her, bent over for a moment, rain-soaked and mud-smeared. Then he straightened up, staring at them by the light of a lamp on a chair, and Beaver saw that he was Kit Markley.

"Well, don't just stand there!" Kit said. "Lend us a hand! We've got to haul everything out of here before this shanty washes away!"

Beaver had never felt more surprised in his life than he did as he and Wally helped Kit carry the table out and off among the trees to a place above the reach of the flooded creek. Kit here and helping Aggie Moss was something that didn't seem to make sense.

Aggie accompanied them carrying the lamp. By its light, Beaver saw that a sort of shelter had been rigged for Aggie's little sister, who was sitting under the mattress from the bed, which had been propped up by a couple of sticks. The little girl was wrapped in a blanket and seemed to be all right.

Kit and Aggie had already taken the bed apart and brought it to safety here. It looked as though they had managed to rescue the shanty's few other scant belongings, also. But, as soon as the table was put down, Kit rushed away, calling, "I'll bring you that last chair, Aggie!"

"I'd better go and see he gets back here all right," Wally said. However, he paused for a moment to wriggle out of his jacket, which he bundled about Aggie. "You need this more than I do," Wally told her.

He went after Kit. Aggie stood holding the lamp. All about them in the darkness people were milling around and calling to each other. From what Beaver could judge, everybody in the little shantytown had been driven out by the rising water.

"Listen, Aggie," he said, "how come Kit Markley is here helping you?"

"What?" Aggie said. It seemed hard for her to think, as she looked at the Moss family's few sodden, mud-smeared things. "Kit? Why, he showed up this morning, wanting to give me some money, too. I wouldn't take it, though, because I still had some of yours left. And I'm sorry, Beaver, I just couldn't find anything to sell at that junk pile last night, so I can't pay you back yet. But I'll make some money, some way, and do it as soon as possible."

"That doesn't matter, Aggie," Beaver told her.

Billy Moss had crawled in under the mattress for shelter from the rain.

"Kit came along again tonight just after it got dark," Aggie went on. "He said that he was worried about us because the creek was rising, and that we had better move out of our place right away. I had already decided the same thing, but I don't think Billy and I could have managed to do it without his help."

It looked as though Kit Markley had figured out for himself what was the right thing to do, and had done it. Beaver was willing to give him full credit for this, though it didn't even up what Kit had done about the bike.

Mr. Markley must be notified at once that his son was safe. Beaver started to tell Aggie he must leave and hurry to the Markley house. Then he discovered that she was crying again.

"I guess this is the finish of everything for us," Aggie said drearily. "We haven't got any place else where we can go. The charity people will come for us sure, now, and take Billy and Jennie."

Beaver tried in vain to think of something to say that might comfort her. She was probably right, he thought. They couldn't stay out in the open on such a night. The charity people would have to take care of them.

Then Billy Moss suddenly scrambled out from under the mattress, crying, "Jennie's rag doll!" He ran off into the darkness.

"Stop him!" Aggie cried. "He's too little. He mustn't go back just for a doll!"

Beaver ran after the little boy. He found himself in the scary darkness again, with the water rising above his knees, racing hard and fast, and plowed through it, shouting, "Billy, wait!"

Almost at once he had a feeling of being lost, of not knowing where the Moss shanty was.

Suddenly Wally was beside him, grabbing his arm. "Get back, Beave!" he cried. "We've done all we can!"

But Beaver hurriedly told him about Billy Moss. Then Wally stood indecisively for a moment. "Gosh, I don't know. The water is pretty high. Going after him, if he is in trouble, is a job for a grown-up—"

"I don't think there is time to get a grown-up to hunt for him!" Beaver said.

Then a streak of lightning showed the Moss shanty in the near distance, and the little boy going into it. Wally said, "You're right, Beave. I'll get him out of there. And you stay right here!"

He plunged away. But Beaver, afraid Wally couldn't handle it alone, could not stand still. He tried to follow his brother. The water was almost up to his waist now, with the roar of the storm-swollen creek frighteningly close, almost as loud as the thunder overhead.

Beaver had to struggle to stay on his feet. The force of the water that had overflowed the bank, flooding the shanties, was very strong.

He pushed on. Where was Wally? Beaver called anxiously to him, but heard no reply.

Another flash of lightning revealed Billy Moss coming out of the shanty again with a doll held high above his head with both hands. The water

was almost up to the little boy's chin. He suddenly went sideways and under as it swept him away.

Beaver lunged toward the youngster, but too late. Somebody splashed into the water, downstream from him, and he heard Kit cry out, "I've got him!"

Kit had seen Billy by that flash of lightning, also, Beaver realized.

Wally shouted, "Where are you?" From the sound of his voice, Wally was even farther down the creek bank, and it seemed the force of the raging current must have pushed him in that direction.

Beaver struggled toward them. He heard Kit cry, "I can't swim—!"

"Hold on!" Wally called. "I'll get you out!"

Thunder crashed again, and Beaver did not hear any more. He struggled on, the darkness so thick he did not know in which direction he was going.

All at once the water about him became more shallow. Beaver did not understand it. He ran faster, calling, "Wally—?"

Wally made some response, but Beaver could not figure where he was. Then Aggie came splashing to stand beside Beaver. She still had her lamp and lifted it as high as she could, with its feeble light spreading for a little distance all about them.

Then Beaver saw Wally.

In water that was chest-deep on him, Wally had his arms about both Aggie's brother and Kit Markley. He was holding them up and trying to drag the pair to safety.

Beaver discovered that he and Aggie were standing on a low ridge a little back from the bank. The creek had not yet risen high enough to cover the ridge very deeply.

Wally was no more than about fifty feet away, a little upstream from Beaver. He was standing on the flooded bank and wasn't managing to make any headway in his effort to drag the two with him out of the water. The force of the current was pushing them sideways toward the frothing tumult of the creek itself.

Beaver's heart thudded painfully as he realized what was liable to happen.

Wally could let go and save himself. He was a strong swimmer. But Beaver knew Wally would never do that.

If he hung onto those two, though, all of them would be swept away.

There was only one thing to do, and it had to be done in a hurry. Beaver tore off his jacket and threw it aside. He said, "Aggie, don't let your lamp go out!"

Then he took two long steps into quickly deepening water and began to swim as hard and as fast as he could. Maybe he could reach them in time, but Beaver did not know whether he could help out if he did. He meant to do his very best, though—and if Wally was shoved into the creek, Beaver was going to be right beside him.

13
A Witness
for Wally

Beaver had to swim against the current. For a couple of moments he did not think he would ever make it. He thought that the flood's force would sweep him away before he ever reached them.

Dad had seen to it that both boys were pretty good swimmers. It was his belief that every boy should be able to take care of himself in the water. When Beaver felt the racing current start to push him sideways and back, he put out added effort, fought harder than he had ever fought before, and somehow he made it.

That is, he bumped against Wally, who gasped, "Here, take hold of this little kid, quick!"

Beaver managed to get an arm about Billy Moss. He then tried to find bottom with his toes and couldn't.

"Head for the light, Beave," Wally said. "I'll be right behind you."

It meant another struggle as Beaver started toward the light of Aggie's lamp, which suddenly seemed to have grown a lot stronger and to have taken on an odd sort of reddish color.

Aggie's brother was squirming feebly and crying. Beaver thrashed with his free arm, trying to swim.

The current was pushing against him from behind now, and Beaver had a moment of fearing he couldn't get free of its grip. But Wally was there, as promised, pulling Kit Markley along with him. Wally put a hand on Beaver's shoulder, shoving him toward the ridge where Aggie stood.

"Take it easy, Beave," Wally said. "We're going to make it okay."

Beaver struggled on. All at once he felt something solid under his feet and lurched out of the water, half-carrying Billy Moss. Beaver kept going until he reached high ground.

Billy Moss was weeping. "I lost Jennie's doll!"

Beaver grunted at this. He had lost both his cap and jacket, but didn't mind as long as everybody was safe. He turned anxiously to his brother who struggled along with Kit. He said, "Are you all right, Wally?"

"Sure," Wally replied. "I'll bet I catch it from Mom and Dad, though, letting you get mixed up in all of this."

Beaver had a feeling he would catch it, also. But this didn't seem to matter very much when measured against what could have happened.

Then he realized the reddish light was growing stronger all the time. Beaver looked about trying to find out where it was coming from. He cried, "Look! The Markley house is on fire!"

The people at the shanties were noticing it, also, and were beginning to shout and head in that direction. The whole lower half of the house was ablaze, with a crackling of flames that was becoming louder than the roar of the creek.

Kit gasped. "Mama! Papa! Maybe they're inside and can't get out!"

He started to run toward the house.

Beaver said, "Somebody has got to turn in an alarm!"

And he immediately remembered two things: the mud slide across the drive, so that Mr. Markley couldn't get his car out, and also that the phone at the burning house was not working.

"I'll go and do it!" Beaver cried.

He began to run through drizzling rain, along the margin of the creek, heading for the bridge. Wally shouted after him, "I'll see if there's anything I can do at that house!"

This side of the bridge, Beaver clawed his way up the bank of the ravine. It was very muddy, and he slipped a couple of times, almost sliding back. But Beaver kept going. He reached the bridge and ran across it.

The fire was a great red glare behind him now, and it seemed somebody certainly ought to see it and phone the fire department. But the street beyond the bridge was deserted, with only a few houses, none of them showing any lights. Beaver ran on, water squishing in his shoes, lungs beginning to burn, and legs wobbling.

He cut across a vacant lot, stumbling through more mud. There wasn't a signal box anywhere close so that he could turn in an alarm. He would have to run all the way to the station.

Beaver came out on the street where the fire station was located. Its doors were open, with light pouring out, and everything was quiet there, so nobody else had yet reported that the Markley house was burning.

He staggered the last block and turned in through those open doors, to see Captain Gus sitting at his desk reading a newspaper, with General dozing on the floor.

"Fire! Captain Gus!" Beaver gasped. "The Markley house—at the hollow—!"

Captain Gus started, peering at him over his glasses. "Now, Beaver," he said, "this isn't any night to be sending us on another wild-goose chase!"

Then he caught himself, peering hard. "Land sakes, boy, you're soaked to the skin! What happened?"

Beaver grabbed at Captain Gus's arm. He pulled him past the big pumper truck, out onto the sidewalk, then pointed. "See for yourself!" Beaver wheezed.

The glow from the fire was an ominous red smudge against the dark clouds that still hung low in the sky.

"Glory be!" Captain Gus exclaimed.

He turned and rushed back inside, shouting, "Everybody out! We're rolling, on a big one!"

Things happened very fast, then—gongs clanging and bells ringing, firemen shooting down the pole through the hole in the ceiling, grabbing at helmets and slickers and leaping onto the truck, whose motor came to life with an explosive roar.

General, barking in wild excitement, sprang to his place beside the driver. Captain Gus wrapped

a blanket about Beaver and lifted him up beside
General, then crowded next to him. "Let's go!"
he cried.

The truck streaked out of the station, siren
beginning to wail almost in Beaver's ear, gong
clanging, red blinker sweeping the street before
them, General barking continuously.

Beaver had always wanted to ride the truck to
a fire. He was certainly getting his wish tonight.

They rushed back along the route he had taken
to reach the station, the big truck careening
around corners, throwing Beaver first against
General, then against Captain Gus. They roared
across the bridge above the creek and along the
street above the hollow, where tires screamed as
the truck slid to a stop.

All of the Markley house was on fire now. It
was like a great glaring torch in the darkness.
Captain Gus studied it for a moment, lips tight.

"Old house and burning fast," he remarked.
"I don't think there's much we can do."

He shouted an order, though: "Couple to that

hydrant up at the next corner and start laying hose. It'll take all we've got to reach down there."

Captain Gus was right. All the firemen could do was keep the blaze from spreading. They managed to save the garage and the big Markley car in the driveway.

Beaver stood looking on. Wally was beside him, also wrapped in a blanket provided from the fire truck.

Kit was standing with his mother nearby. Mrs. Markley had insisted on hugging both Beaver and Wally after hearing how her son had been pulled from the floodwater. Beaver noticed that Kit wasn't claiming any credit at all for what had happened at the creek.

Mr. Markley came to shake hands with Beaver and Wally, squeezing hard. He told how the fire had started. Going down into the cellar he had slipped on the steep stairs and had almost taken a bad fall. Grabbing at a stair rail to save himself, he had dropped the lantern.

It had smashed, spilling oil. Fire from the lantern's wick, spreading through the oil, had reached the cellar walls, which had burned so fast that Mr. Markley had barely managed to make it back up the stairs again. Then there was nothing he could do other than to find Kit's mother and hurry her out of the house.

The servants had been given the night off. All of them had been gone since early evening.

Mr. Markley also said, "The light was on in the cellar. I think you and Kit must have left it on last night, Beaver, when you were at work there."

Beaver thought he was probably right. He said, "I'm awfully sorry this had to happen to you, Mr. Markley."

"I'm not sorry at all," Mr. Markley replied, looking toward the house as the roof fell in with a shuddering roar. "I am beginning to think it is a good thing. I'll build a new house here, one that isn't big and gloomy, the kind of house Kit's mother wants."

This would seem to mean that Kit was going

to be around for quite a while.

Mr. Markley said, finally, "I'll never forget what you two boys did tonight. I mean to do something in return to show the deep appreciation of Mrs. Markley and myself."

"Ah, that's all right, sir," Wally told him. "You don't need to do anything."

"I disagree," Mr. Markley said. "And I will think of something."

Ward and June Cleaver appeared, then, and Mom came hurrying to look both of them over. She bent down to Beaver, hands shaking a little as she put them on his arms while anxiously studying him.

He said, "I'm all right, Mom. Honest!"

"Yes, I can see you are," Mom said, with a deep, relieved sigh. "But you might catch cold. We ought to take you and Wally right home—"

"Gee, no!" he protested. "Please! Let us stay until the fire is out!"

Dad, coming along also, said, "I think you should give in this one time, June. Such an exciting fire doesn't happen very often. I feel the boys should be allowed to watch it."

"Hmph!" Mom said. "What you really mean is that wild horses couldn't drag *you* away from it!"

But she laughed, and they stood together for a while, looking on.

Then Dad moved to join Mr. Markley and several others. They started talking about the people who had been flooded out in the hollow.

"It is time to end the disgrace of those shanties," Dad said. "And even though it isn't the town's responsibility, there must be something we can do to provide such people decent places in which to live."

"I agree with you, Ward," Mr. Markley said. "And as for the Moss youngsters that my son and yours tried to help, I mean to take care of them personally."

The rain had stopped and the clouds were starting to break up. Quite a crowd had gathered by now. Beaver noticed Aggie Moss moving about, telling everybody that he and Wally had saved her brother's life. He wished she would stop doing that.

So did Wally. "Doggone it, everybody is looking at us," Wally muttered. "I think we ought to go home now, Beave. I'm tired of standing around in these wet clothes."

"So am I," Beaver decided. Anyway, the fire was nearly out.

They started toward the street. But they had waited too long, for Mr. Grimsby had appeared on the scene. His son Sylvester was with him, blinking through his thick glasses.

Mr. Grimsby stared at Wally, and all at once was as angry as when he had ordered Wally, Lumpy, and Eddie away from his garage.

"What about that car of mine that you took out and wrecked, young man?" Mr. Grimsby demanded loudly. "This is pretty brazen of you, I must say, coming to watch a fire and have a good time when you ought to be confined at home because of what you did!"

Wally cried, "Mr. Grimsby, I told you I didn't

have anything to do with what happened to your car!"

"I say you did!" Mr. Grimsby snapped. "I say you took it from behind my garage at about eight last night and drove it down to the river road and wrecked it! And we're going to settle things right now, with no more delay. I see your father standing over there. Either he pays up or I call the police!"

Beaver felt sick and scared for Wally. With everything else happening so fast, he had forgotten all about the trouble over Mr. Grimsby's car. So, it was evident, had Wally, who wore a pale, pinched look.

Dad would have to pay Mr. Grimsby now, Beaver thought. And Wally would have to wash dishes for a long time in order to save enough to pay him back.

Then Aggie Moss shoved past Beaver and stopped to face Mr. Grimsby, glaring at him.

"You stop saying such things!" Aggie cried. "Wally Cleaver didn't have anything at all to do with taking that car away from your garage at the time you said!"

Mr. Grimsby stared at her in return. "Hush up, girl," he said. "You don't know what you're talking about."

"I do know!" Aggie said. "Because I was right there, going through your trash pile, hoping I could find something that I might sell. I couldn't, though. You must not ever throw anything away if it's worth even a penny!"

She glanced around toward Beaver then for a second. "I promised I wouldn't ever snitch on anybody again," Aggie said. "But I've just got to do it one more time."

Facing Mr. Grimsby anew, she drew a deep breath and hurried on. "I saw who came along and got in a car and drove it away from behind your garage about eight o'clock. It wasn't Wally Cleaver!"

Beaver and Wally, both listening in amazement, saw somebody suddenly start to back away from Aggie, face the color of wet ashes, blinking hard as though he was about to cry.

"There's the one who did it!" Aggie cried, and pointed straight at Mr. Grimsby's own son, Sylvester Grimsby.

14
Beaver Makes
Up His Mind

It was just past noon, the following day, with a warm sun out and everything slowly drying. Wally and Beaver, back from church, were sitting on the front porch, waiting for Mom to announce that Sunday dinner was ready.

Beaver said, "Wally, are we really heroes?"

"Nah, I don't think so," Wally replied. "Maybe Kit is a hero, though, because he tried to get Billy Moss out of the water even though he knew he couldn't swim."

Beaver thought about this and had to agree that Wally was probably right. "But Mom and Dad seem to think we're heroes," he pointed out.

"Well, they're our folks, and they want to be

proud of us," Wally said. "So I guess it doesn't hurt for them to think that, as long as we don't get big-headed and start thinking the same thing ourselves."

Beaver decided Wally was right, again. He said, "It was sure nice of you not to be mad at Sylvester."

Wally said, "Well, the poor guy had been through enough already, knowing he had wrecked his father's car but being too afraid to say so."

Sylvester had broken down and cried, confessing that he had taken the car out not only on Friday night, when Aggie Moss had seen him, but a number of times prior to that. Like Wally, he had wanted a lot to have a car of his own but Mr. Grimsby wouldn't even listen to his pleas, so he had taken to driving the heap without his father's knowledge. And he had wrecked it on Friday night.

Mr. Grimsby had apologized to both Dad and Wally before he and his son had gone away from the Markleys' together.

"I hope his dad won't be too hard on him," Wally continued.

Beaver said, "You'll soon have a car of your own, Wally, after what is going to happen this summer!"

Wally was going to spend his summer vacation in Montana working on a ranch owned by Mr. Markley's brother. This was the way Kit's father had found to show his appreciation. He had called his brother long-distance this morning, and everything was all arranged.

"You'll get to ride horses and round up cattle, and do all sorts of keen things!" Beaver said.

"Just so I don't have to wash any dishes!" Wally said, and both of them laughed. There wouldn't have to be any more worry about him having to go to work at the Busy Bee restaurant.

Mom hadn't been very much in favor at first of Wally going off to Montana, but Dad had said, "It will do him a world of good, June. Bob Markley's brother has promised to look after him personally. Wally will come back bigger and heavier and morc grown-up from the experience."

"I'm not sure I want him that way," Mom had said. "But I know it is going to happen in time even if he stays at home, so I won't object any longer."

"Gosh, Wally, I wish I could go with you!" Beaver told his brother.

"Your chance will probably come before very long," Wally said.

Beaver hoped so. He knew that he couldn't go to Montana this summer, because he wasn't old enough. He decided not to say anything more about it, because to do so might sound as though he were envious of Wally, and not as pleased as he could be for him.

Beaver's problem was what to do about Kit Markley. He didn't know yet how he would solve that problem.

The Markleys were going to stay in an apartment until their new home was built. As they had promised, they were looking after the Moss children. The charity people didn't mind and had no intention of separating Aggie from her brother and sister. Mr. Moss had already been located by the police and was being brought back, with the promise that a job would be found for him.

It was certainly strange the way things had worked out, Beaver thought. He had tried to help Aggie, and in turn she had cleared Wally of the charge against him.

It had been a nightmare but was now all over —except what Beaver was going to do about Kit.

Wally spoke again. "I'm not going to get a car with the money I'll make this summer. Not right away, at least. I'll save it and work summer after next, too. By then I'll be a junior in high school— I'll have a driver's license and I can get a good car, not a beat-up old heap."

Beaver was surprised. "I thought you wanted one real bad," he said.

"Well, I do," Wally replied. "But I've also been doing some thinking. Dad says there is a right way and a wrong way to do everything. What I tried just caused a lot of trouble, so it must have been wrong. Wanting to own a heap when I couldn't drive it was wrong, too. Waiting until I'm ready sounds a lot more sensible."

Beaver thought this over, also. "I guess that's true, Wally," he agreed, though doubtfully. "But if it was me I don't think I could do any waiting. Do you s'pose you feel that way because you're more grown-up than I am?"

"Maybe so," Wally replied.

It seemed to Beaver his brother was considerably more grown-up as a result of all that had happened, though he didn't feel much different himself and had a moment of wondering if he ever would.

It would take time to find out, Beaver thought. And he was curious about something else. "Listen, Wally, why did you stand around under the trees at the library park on Friday night?" he asked.

Wally hesitated. Beaver continued, "I won't tell anybody, cross my heart!"

"Well, you be sure that you don't," Wally said. "I heard a girl would be heading for the library that night, and I figured that I would step out real casual like and bump into her when she came along. She didn't show up, though, so I had to stand around for nothing."

"If you wanted to see her, why didn't you just go to her house and ring the doorbell?" Beaver demanded.

"You don't do it that way," Wally said. "You've got to find out first whether she's interested in you. You've got to be very casual about it, so you won't wind up feeling like a boob, with everybody laughing at you, in case she gives you a brush-off."

"It all sounds mighty silly to me," Beaver said. "I don't know why you have to be interested in girls anyway!"

Wally laughed. "You'll be getting interested in them yourself—but not for a while yet," he said.

Dad came out of the house. "Dinner is almost ready, men, so don't stray off," he said. "I must eat in a hurry and then run."

He was going to a meeting where plans would be made to tear down the shanties in the hollow,

and to find homes for those who had lived there.

Dad glanced at Wally, started slightly, and said, "Son, let me have a good look at you."

He took Wally's chin between thumb and forefinger, turned his head a little, then went on, "Wally, you're getting a little fuzzy-cheeked."

"Gee whiz, Dad!" Wally cried. "No kidding?"

"No kidding at all," Dad replied. "Your first shave will be due before very long—but not today, if you don't mind. I think your mother has had about all she can take for the time being. And by the time you return from Montana, I'll bet you'll be using a razor almost every week."

"Oh, boy!" Wally said. "I've got to go and take a look. Then, right after dinner I'll find Lumpy and Eddie. Am I ever going to have things to tell them!"

He rushed inside. Dad glanced at Beaver with a smile and a wink, and followed him.

Beaver had a sudden feeling of loneliness. Wally would be gone all summer, and would be changed when he came back. Beaver had a sense of Wally moving ahead in the world and leaving him behind. He did not like it.

But he didn't have a chance to think much about this, for Kit Markley came along, and he had the bicycle—pushing it, instead of riding.

Beaver felt a painful twinge at sight of the bike. He hadn't been doing any thinking about it, particularly, but would have thought it had been destroyed, because the Markleys had lost just about everything else in the fire. But it hadn't been destroyed and was a reminder of what Kit had done to him.

Kit stopped on the walk. He said hesitantly, "Hi!"

"Hello," Beaver replied, reminding himself he had to get along with Kit. Wally might not get to go to Montana if he didn't. It was going to be hard to do, though, even when he reminded himself, also, that Kit had shown there was good stuff in him by helping Aggie, offering her his share of the money from the bottles, and courageously attempting to rescue little Billy Moss.

"I told Captain Gus I was the one who turned in that false alarm, and you didn't have anything to do with it," Kit said.

Beaver supposed this meant he could go to the fire station again if he wanted to.

"I also told my folks I don't want a tutor any more," Kit said. "I want to go to school here starting next fall. They said it's okay, because you'll be there to help me get to know the guys and learn what to do."

"Sure," Beaver said. "I'll do that."

"Maybe we can do a lot of things together this summer, too," Kit suggested.

"I guess so," Beaver agreed.

He couldn't help it if the prospect of doing things with Kit didn't excite him very much. And Kit, moistening his lips, went on, as though he had put off what he must say next as long as he could, "I—I want to tell you about this bicycle, now—"

Words came from him with a rush, then. He had talked about the bicycle at home, but his

mother hadn't understood that Beaver was working to buy it. Mrs. Markley had said Kit should
have a reward for all of his hard work with the
bottles. She had gone to Mr. Hallam's shop yesterday and had bought it as a surprise for him.

Kit had been very upset, knowing what Beaver
must be thinking. "I don't want the bike," he said.
"I don't even know how to ride it!"

"Well, it isn't hard to learn how," Beaver said.
"I'll show you."

"No!" Kit said, and went on talking.

He had discovered this morning that the bike
was in the Markley garage, undamaged, and had
decided at once what he must do with it. His
father had agreed immediately. So had his mother
when she understood.

"We all want you to have it," Kit said. "Beaver,
take the bike. Please!"

Beaver realized this was how the Markleys had
decided to express their appreciation to him for
last night. But, at the same time, he remembered
what Wally had said, that there was a right way

and a wrong way to do everything.

"I can't take it, Kit," he replied. "You see, I was going to earn the bike and that's still the way it has to be, even though I don't guess there's much chance for me ever to do any such thing now."

Beaver thought for a moment of the bottles still in the Markley cellar, but nobody would ever be able to collect on them now.

He knew his answer was right, though. He knew that if he didn't earn the bike the way he had planned from the beginning, it wouldn't have very much meaning for him.

"Maybe there is a chance!" Kit said. "My father was saying this morning that he is going to hire somebody, right away, to fill up that old mine he dug. We'll ask him to hire us!"

"Gosh!" Beaver said. "You think he would?"

"Sure! So you can have the bike right now, and pay for it later," Kit said. "I'll leave it here—"

"No," Beaver said. "That's real nice of you, Kit, but I don't want the bike until it's all paid for."

This, he thought, was right, also.

Maybe, Beaver told himself, he had done some growing up, too, these last few days. He felt a new sort of determination and steadiness in himself. It was a good feeling.

"You keep the bike, Kit," he said.

"Okay," Kit agreed reluctantly.

"When it's all mine, I'll show you how to ride," Beaver continued. "Maybe you can get one, too."

"I sure will!" Kit exclaimed. "I'll work hard and save my money, and I'll buy one just like it!"

Things had never meant much to him before, but, the way his eyes were shining now, Beaver had an idea that a bike he had worked hard to own would mean something. It would mean plenty.

Mom came out, then. "Hello, Kit," she said. "Wouldn't you like to have dinner with us?"

"Gee, Mrs. Cleaver, that would be swell!" Kit said.

Mom smiled, with a dimple showing in her cheek. "Perhaps you aren't going to be another Eddie after all," she said. "Beaver will show you where to wash up for dinner, Kit."

Beaver realized his feeling of loneliness at Wally's being away all summer was gone. He would miss Wally, of course, but not as much as he had feared.

"We can do a lot of things, as soon as we both have bikes," he told Kit as they went in together. "And listen, Mom and Dad and I will be going to the mountains for a trip in July. We'll camp out and fish and hike and swim and all sorts of other swell stuff. I'll bet we could fix it up for you to go along, if you want to."

Kit swallowed hard. "That would be wonderful!" he said.

It was going to be a real good summer, Beaver thought. And Wally wasn't the only one who would be bigger and heavier and more grown-up when it was over. Beaver had a feeling that Wally was going to be plenty surprised at the change in his brother when he got back from Montana!

Whitman
CLASSICS

Five Little Peppers Midway

Freckles

Wild Animals I Have Known

Rebecca of Sunnybrook
Farm

Alice in Wonderland

Mrs. Wiggs of the
Cabbage Patch

Fifty Famous Fairy Tales

Rose in Bloom

Eight Cousins

Little Women

Little Men

Five Little Peppers and
How They Grew

Robinson Crusoe

Treasure Island

Heidi

The Call of the Wild

Tom Sawyer

Beautiful Joe

Adventures of Sherlock Holmes

Here are some of the best-loved stories of all time. Delightful ... intriguing ... never-to-be-forgotten tales that you will read again and again. Start your own home library of WHITMAN CLASSICS so that you'll always have exciting books at your finger tips.

Whitman

REG. U.S. PAT. OFF.

Whitman ADVENTURE and MYSTERY Books

Adventure Stories for GIRLS and BOYS...

New Stories About Your Television Favorites...

TIMBER TRAIL RIDERS

The Long Trail North
The Texas Tenderfoot
The Luck of Black Diamond

THE BOBBSEY TWINS

In the Country
Merry Days Indoors and Out
At the Seashore

DONNA PARKER

In Hollywood
At Cherrydale
Special Agent
On Her Own
A Spring to Remember
Mystery at Arawak

TROY NESBIT SERIES

The Forest Fire Mystery
The Jinx of Payrock Canyon
Sand Dune Pony

Dr. Kildare
   Assigned to Trouble

Janet Lennon
   And the Angels
   Adventure at Two Rivers
   Camp Calamity

Walt Disney's Annette
   The Mystery at Smugglers' Cove
   The Desert Inn Mystery
   Sierra Summer
   The Mystery at Moonstone Bay

The Lennon Sisters
   Secret of Holiday Island

Leave It to Beaver

Ripcord

The Beverly Hillbillies

Lassie
   The Mystery at Blackberry Bog

Lucy
   The Madcap Mystery

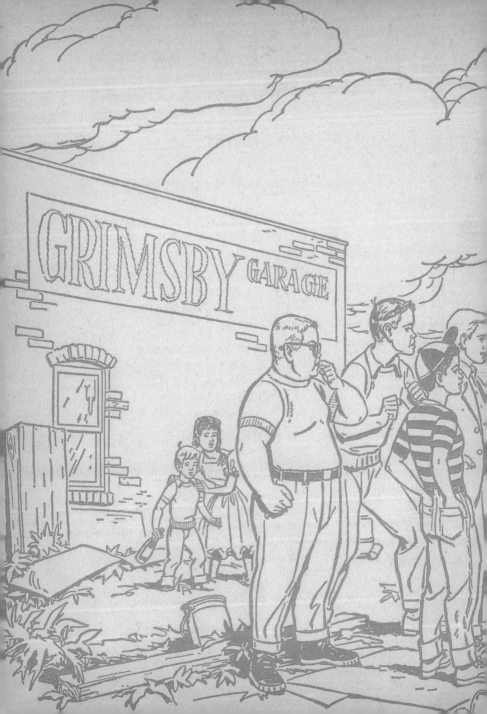